# SWING SONG

By Daniel Cole

This book is a work of fiction. Any references to historical events, real people, or real places are used fictitiously. Other names, characters, places, and events are products of the author's imagination, and any resemblance to actual events or places or persons, living or dead, is entirely coincidental.

Copyright © 2018 Daniel Cole
All rights reserved.

**ISBN:** 9798883599056
**Imprint:** Independently published

I wrote this story as a tribute to America's finest: *The first responders*. Immense gratitude to the friends and family who made this possible, I will never be able to thank you enough.

*For Steve*

It was difficult to see with the blood in her eyes. Her once blonde hair was now dyed red and had become a tangled mess in front of her face. Her heart was thundering. Her breathing was labored and elevated. The massive gash on her forehead was steadily streaming blood across her face and was dripping quietly onto the floor. *How...* she thought, *how did I get here? Where am I?* The room she was in was devoid of any light and was uncomfortably cold. A smell of mildew and dust hung in the air. She struggled to stand and nearly fell over before realizing her hands and feet were bound to a sturdy metal chair. The daze of confusion was fading and now was quickly being replaced with paralyzing fear.

"*Oh my God!*" she cried, "*Where the hell am I!*"

She began to scream for help but could only hear the echo of her own tormented voice bouncing off the room's invisible walls. She strained her neck to see her surroundings, but the room was darker than a starless night, and it was impossible to orient herself. She thrashed at the restraints again. They were tight knots and were constricting the circulation to her hands and feet. The fear grew more intense.

She continued to struggle against her bonds. She wondered how she had got there. She couldn't remember a thing. Her head felt like someone had stuck a hot poker into her skull and every time she struggled, the pain flashed like white fire and made her wince.

*How did this happen?* She pondered the question with her limited consciousness. *Ok, I was with Tammy after work, and we were drinking and… Am I dreaming?* The pain in her head was like nothing she had ever felt before. She had once fallen off a galloping horse and cracked three vertebrae, but somehow, this was worse. It was nearly unbearable, and it spoke a horrible truth to her; *No,* she realized. *This is no dream.*

She screamed for help until her strength faded and her voice went hoarse. Defeated, the terrified young woman hung her head and began to sob. She cried and thought of her parents and how she wouldn't see them, or her new dalmatian puppy again. She regretted not getting married and starting a family. A whirlwind of regrets and missed opportunities circled her mind as she lamented her situation. She cried out of agony and remorse, but most of all, she cried out of dread. The thought of death was just too much to bear. She continued to cry alone in the dark.

Her grief was interrupted when suddenly she heard a sound. It startled her out of her sorrow, and she strained at the darkness trying to hear it again. Her ears were acting as eyes in the blackness that enveloped her, searching for the source. A minute had passed when she did not hear anything except her own heart pounding with alarm. *Did I imagine it?* she thought. *I probably have some sort of concussion. That doesn't help.*

She was about to dismiss it to anxiety and fear, but then she heard it… *again.*

Her body went rigid, and she strained against the ropes. The noise was not more than a few feet away from her this time. It sounded, approximately, to be directly to her right. Mute from shock, she turned her aching head and she stared into the abyss, searching for any clue of the origin of the sound.

A foul smell filled her nostrils, a stench like meat that had turned and then began to rot. The noise grew closer. It sounded like heavy chains being dragged across the floor, but as soon as it started, it stopped again. The woman began to hyperventilate and was becoming hypoxic. Panic was taking over. Her mind raced at the possibilities of what it could be or what was about to happen to her. The absolute terror filled her veins with ice and the adrenaline was coursing through her in torrents, but she was still unable to move. She couldn't talk. She could hardly think.

Her ears rang loudly, and her muscle fibers twitched uncontrollably. Her entire nervous system was in overdrive and screamed for her to run, yet she sat as still as a rabbit hiding from a predator. While her fear reached its pinnacle, the sound began again, closer than ever, and the vile odor grew increasingly stronger. She suddenly felt the chill of her hair rising on the back of her neck. The goosebumps traveled throughout her body and into her very soul.

She could feel the hot breath on her cheek. The putrid smell. Hear the soft breathing. Though she could not see it, she knew it was there, the reason that she was now a captive. It was inches away from her face, hidden in the dark.

# ONE

Eleven-year-old Santina Shard sat on the swing, as she did most days, counting the fence posts across the playground. It was a Saturday so there was no school and she was alone. The sky was overcast, and the air was warm, but she still had her dirty zebra stripe coat on. She didn't go anywhere without it. Grandma gave it to her when Grandpa was still alive but they're both gone now. She liked to swing. To her, it was the only thing in this world that made sense. As she counted the posts, the swing creaked and groaned audibly but she didn't mind. A symphony of sound echoed from the old swing set, creating a unique and beautiful song that Santina knew inside and out. It was a song that she was completely familiar with and utterly at peace when she heard it. It was better than the noises at home anyway. Momma's noises. *His* noises.

She continued to swing when a group of kids walked by on the sidewalk parallel to the swing set. She recognized them from her school, Kady Elementary. One of the kids, a boy, yelled excitedly to the others, saying, "there she is! there's the retard!" The kids at her school were very mean. They were always calling her names like "stupid" and "retard" just because she couldn't speak very well. She stuttered and had problems enunciating and it led to terrible torment from her peers. Momma said it was God's punishment for being the reason why daddy left. She was ostracized and always ate lunch alone, no one ever wanted to play with her during recess and she yearned for a friend. The teachers would tell her to try and make friends, but she couldn't do it. She even once tried to join a group of girls that were playing on the jungle gym as a last-ditch effort to improve her social standing. It resulted in disaster.

The ringleader of the girls, Sally Mosenteen, was atop the jungle gym when Santina approached. Before she could even greet the group, she heard Sally say, "Oh look!" loud enough for the entire playground to hear.

"It's Santina Shard, the Retard!"

The playground erupted in laughter and Santina stopped in her tracks. Paralyzed with fear and embarrassment, Santina was unable to move. Even as the onslaught of vicious remarks and ridicule bombarded her from the faces of the children on the playground, Santina remained frozen. "What's the matter dummy?" Sally sneered, "why don't you say something?"

Santina shut her eyes as tight as she could and covered her ears and screamed but couldn't drown out the noise. "Retard Shard! Retard Shard! Retard Shard!" they chanted in unison as a crowd would cheer for their favorite sports team. The humiliation was unbearable, and it finally ended when a teacher, Mr. Harrison, the school's gym teacher, put a stop to the cacophony of insults with a thunderous, "That's enough!" The children immediately ceased their jeers. "You should all be ashamed of yourselves," continued Mr. Harrison. "That is no way to treat a friend and classmate! We do not condone such behavior at this school."

"She's not our friend!" Sally retorted. The comment drew a few snickers from other kids. Mr. Harrison glanced sharply in her direction. "Miss Mosenteen, I highly suggest that you be quiet before I call your parents." Sally began to protest but decided against it. Mr. Harrison grunted contently and then escorted Santina off the playground and back into the school.

"Thank you, Mr. Harrison," Santina said shyly as they walked. Tears welled in her eyes, and she wiped them with the sleeve of her coat. Her speech impediment was very apparent to Mr. Harrison as they spoke. *Ffffannk you Mr. Haawison.*

"Santina, you need to not worry about the opinions of these kids. You have one of the highest grades in your class. You are not an idiot by any means," said Mr. Harrison. She looked up at him and he smiled broadly at her. "Keep your chin up," he said, "it will get better". It was the only kindness that she received since she started the fifth grade.

"Hey stupid!"

The voice reeled Santina back from her memories of the playground incident nearly two months ago, and it forced her to where she was on the swing set with a new group of bullies.

"Hey retard, I'm talking to you!" shouted the boy again. Santina glanced shyly over as she continued swinging and saw the boy was Conner Simmons, the meanest boy in her grade. She did not recognize the other kids that were with him but assumed by the toothy grins on their faces, they were there to see Conner in action.

As the group spectated, Simmons walked through the playground entrance and proceeded over to Santina, making a quick stop at a small rock pile, and grabbed a few golf ball sized stones. As soon as he did, he began launching them with great velocity towards her, striking her on her legs and elbow. She covered herself the best she could, but the momentum of the swing kept exposing her body. Over and over, she was hit, and cried out in pain. Conner flung his final missile and struck Santina square in the cheek, causing her to bleed. The shock from the blow dazed Santina and she instinctively leaned backwards away from the pain. The change in direction caused her to tumble out the back of the swing seat and land hard on the ground.

The children laughed and ran off, leaving her in the woodchips underneath the swing. Conner Simmons stayed a moment longer to admire his work and ran to catch up with them.

The momentum of the swing set allowed the seat to swing back and forth as if there were a ghost making it move. The hinges continued to squeak loudly, and she laid there, not moving, listening to the swing sing it eerie song. She never felt so lonely. Why was everyone so mean to her? *What is so wrong with me?* she thought and began to sob quietly. She thought back to Mr. Harrison and his kind words that day on the playground. She wondered when it would get better like Mr. Harrison had promised.

However, Mr. Harrison wasn't there to protect her today. She was by herself. She stood up from the woodchips, sniffled, and brushed herself off. Her long brown hair was matted to the blood on her cheek, and she winced as she pulled the hair from the wound. It was swollen and bruising with a nasty cut in the center. As she was cleaning herself up, she looked around and realized that it was getting late, and the streetlamps were on. The kids had run off to find other children to bully no doubt, and she was glad that they were gone. She wiped the tears from her eyes and climbed back on the swing and began to move as she pumped her legs back and forth, gaining speed and altitude with each new flurry of leg swings until she could go no higher. She was alone again on her swing. She began to count the fence posts again, starting from the left side this time. It was getting late, but she didn't want to go home. Anywhere but there. She knew that HE was there. She would rather face the bullies than see him again, so she sat silently on the swing and swung into the evening. The hinges squeaked.

# TWO

Detective Glenn Blackthorne awoke harshly from his sleep. He was drenched in sweat and glanced at his alarm clock on the bedside table. 2:45 AM. "Christ," he muttered. That was the third night in a row he had that dream, the one where the woman was being burned alive in her trailer. He no doubt had nightmares about it because only about three weeks earlier, that actual incident unfolded in a trailer outside of Tulsa. As a Detective for the Tulsa Police Department, Glenn had been called to investigate the incident.

Glenn rolled over and watched his wife Mary sleeping soundly next to him. *At least I didn't wake her this time,* he thought as he closed his eyes and attempted to fall asleep again, but the sleep never came. He could still smell that damn smoke. That acrid, piercing smell that contained the evil of the deed that had occurred. Frustrated with his inability to rest, Glenn arose from his bed, changed his shirt, put on a robe and slippers, and padded down the carpeted hall to the kitchen. He turned on the kitchen light and put a new filter in the coffee pot and filled the reservoir with water. He then grabbed his favorite Colombian dark roast and looked inside. "Not enough for a full pot," he said, annoyed, and threw it in the trash. He grabbed his wife's favorite brew, some caramel flavored junk, and poured it into the filter and fired the coffee pot up.

He stood there for a while, leaning against the counter with both hands, watching the coffee drip. As the pot hissed and gurgled, he found himself thinking back to the fire. Three weeks ago, he was discussing an unrelated case with a particularly unlikeable county attorney named Paul Facks. Paul was a timid man whose reputation as a pushover in the courtroom preceded him. He also had an irritating slogan of "Paul Facks needs the facts," no doubt an effort to try and be funny, but it usually annoyed the piss out of any officer who had to speak with him. Paul was droning on about case law and Glenn was contemplating jumping out of the office window, when he received a call from his colleague and close friend, Detective Scott Shoemaker.

"Talk to me Scott-dog," Glenn greeted. It was a playful nickname he had given his friend years ago. "Hey Glenn," answered Scott. Glenn knew his friend well enough to know something was wrong. Scott's usually cheerful voice was somber and melancholy.

"What's going on, Scott?"

"I need you to meet me on the southside of the Wabash trailer park. Got a messy one for you to look at."

"What happened?"

"Fire. Got a body too."

"Which trailer?"

"You'll know it when you get here."

Glenn shifted in his chair. He didn't like how this sounded. The Wabash trailer park was, for the most part, a fairly calm area, at least, by law enforcement standards. It has had a reputation for rowdiness and an occasional alcohol related incident, but never any serious crimes. Glenn also didn't like how Scott sounded over the phone. Scott was a veteran detective and had seen the very worst police work had to offer. This one must have bothered him quite a bit. Furthermore, due to a new zoning change, the Wabash trailer park was no longer in the Tulsa PD jurisdiction.

"Scott, Wabash isn't our problem anymore remember? We will have to pass the case on to Sapulpa PD or Sand Springs or whoever the hell is taking over that area."

"Well," Scott responded, "If you would read your damn emails from time to time, you would know that the zoning change doesn't go into effect till September. So, this one is ours, guy."

Glenn sighed. "Alright. I'm on my way. Give me about twenty."

"10-4," said Scott.

Glenn ended the call and checked the time on his phone and looked back up at Paul. "Sorry Paul. Gotta go."

Paul chuckled. "Best of luck Detective and remember, if you bring me a new case, Paul Facks needs the facts!"

With that, Glenn stood and exited the office. Feeling relieved to get away from Paul, he walked to the parking lot and entered his unmarked police cruiser and sat in the driver's seat.

"Fuck you and your luck," he muttered as he started the engine.

Glenn poured a cup of coffee and sat down at the kitchen table. As he sipped, he stared at his Police Academy graduation photo across the hall and recalled how his career had unfolded. Upon graduation from high school, he pursued a career in business and got accepted into the Spears School of Business at Oklahoma State University on an academic scholarship. Try as he might, he didn't enjoy school and dropped out after his first year. Reluctant to work a dead- end job, he enlisted in the Army as a combat medic, much to his father's disappointment. He excelled at his work and within two and a half years of his enlistment, had been promoted to the rank of Sergeant. He was even the youngest soldier in his Battalion to have earned the Army's coveted Expert Field Medical Badge.

After a difficult combat deployment to Afghanistan in 2008, he opted to not re-enlist for a second term and after four years of being away, he returned home to Tulsa. Immediately on return, he felt a sense of camaraderie and brotherhood missing from his daily life. The structure and discipline were cornerstones of life in the military, and now they had suddenly vanished. Though the Army was trying and difficult to navigate, he still missed his friends and the trials they all endured together. He needed to be a part of a team again but was lost in how he would accomplish it.

"Everything alright?" Mary asked, walking into the kitchen. "You're up early." Startled out of his deep thought, Glenn looked up at his wife's tired, concerned face. Her blonde hair was in a messy bun and her big blue eyes were still full of sleep. She was wearing a light pink bathrobe and a pair of matching slippers.

"I'm fine, love," Glenn said. "Couldn't sleep."

Mary nodded and sat down at the table next to him. As Glenn watched her, he couldn't believe how beautiful she was, even when nearly asleep. "You've got a big day today," she said. "What time is the interview?"

Glenn thought for a second before answering. "I have a "pre-interview meeting with the Chief at one, so…yeah. Interview is at two."

Mary smiled. She was so very proud of her husband for doing what he had to do. Not only was he a good man of character but he was a great husband as well. This arson case was very difficult for him and somehow, he pulled through. Now that it was solved, the local news channel wanted to interview him about the case and what had transpired. Much to Glenn's hesitance, he eventually agreed.

They both sat in silence for a few minutes. Mary stood up, "I'm going back to bed," she said, kissing Glenn on the cheek and rubbed her hand across his back. "You're a good man Glenn Blackthorne. You did the right thing." She began back down the hall towards their bedroom but stopped. "Do you think they're going to ask you about Scott?" Mary asked.

"Almost certainly," said Glenn. "There is no way I can get out of this without talking about Scott Shoemaker."

## THREE

At 6:00 AM, Glenn left the kitchen and went upstairs to get ready for work. He shaved his face and took a cold shower. The icy water shocked his system and forced an increase in blood flow throughout his body. Glenn didn't necessarily enjoy the artic plunge, but he considered it to be better than any caffeine source. As he left the shower, he put his towel around his waist and looked at himself in the mirror. He admired at his broad chest and fingered the one-inch scar on his left pectoral, a scar he received from a gang banger who pulled a knife on him while on a domestic assault call. His hand moved down across the right side of his ribs, where another scar, much larger than the one on his chest, was visible. That one he had received from a drunk driver that clipped him with their mirror while he was conducting a traffic stop. He suffered five broken ribs and deep bruising around the gash for weeks.

Finally, he admired the numerous circular scars that adorned his right forearm. He rubbed the faded scars and remembered back to the day he received them. He was called to a home for a welfare check for elderly woman because she had not been seen or heard from by the mail man, whom she normally greeted every morning when he was walking his route. When she stopped meeting him outside and the mailbox became full, the mailman became concerned and called the police.

When Glenn had arrived at the house, there was no answer at the door, but a foul smell was emanating from inside. Recognizing that it was the smell of a deceased person, Glenn opened the door and carefully made his way inside. The smell was awful and hung thick in the air. Glenn called out and proceeded into the home, when out of nowhere, the largest dog that he had ever seen, leaped out of the shadows and bit him on the arm. Thor, the two-hundred-pound cream colored Great Dane, knocked Glenn into the wall and they began to fight for position. As Glenn attempted to grab his sidearm, Thor suddenly let go, possibly sensing that Glenn was not a threat and the four-legged shark doubled back from the hallway where he appeared, as if leading the way. Glenn was beyond irate that the dog had bitten him, and radioed for an extra patrol unit and the ambulance as he left the house and closed the door.

The other officer arrived shortly after, and Glenn advised his back up about the mammoth dog waiting inside the house. When ready, they both re-entered the residence, weapons up. They searched the house, calling out to make their presence known, when they walked into the bedroom where they saw the elderly woman in an advanced state of decay, with Thor standing over her, woofing deeply at them. Thor was forced to live with his dead owner for over a week, surviving on flesh that he removed from her body and the water he found in the toilet. Glenn's arm was on fire from the bite wounds, but after seeing what the poor dog had to endure, Glenn decided to cut him some slack.

Once the body was removed from the house, Glenn was still wary of Thor, even when the giant dog nuzzled his hand and allowed Glenn to pet him. Glenn rarely got emotional when he saw a dead body because he had seen so many of them in his line of work, but the sight of a woman who was so far decayed upset him tremendously. It wasn't that she was dead, it was that she was so alone in the world that she died and began to rot and there was no one to care for her during her last days to notice that she passed. A week later, after the woman's funeral and with the family's permission, Glenn adopted Thor and they have been best buddies ever since. To this day, Glenn wondered why a frail old woman would ever want a dog that was the size of a small cow. Admittingly though, Glenn didn't like it when Thor licked him. It gave him a chill to think that the dog had tasted human before and though it had been years since the incident, Glenn swore he could still smell her on his breath.

As Glenn looked at himself in the mirror, he noticed how his once young features had changed into a grizzled, hardened version of his former self. The stress of the job and the things that he had witnessed were burned into his soul and it took a very serious toll on his body. Wrinkles had formed in his forehead and between his eyebrows, and his joints hurt from countless fights with suspects and criminals. The job was causing him to age rapidly and his physician warned him to take care of his blood pressure before he entered an early grave. The incident with Thor and his rotting owner were only one of a million horrific memories that Glenn wished he could forget, but as anyone who has witnessed the unthinkable knows, those moments live with you forever.

      Glenn left the shower, put on black dress pants, and a white collared shirt. He wore a black suit jacket over the shirt and on his belt, he put his holster and detective's badge over his right hip. He took his Glock 17 9mm pistol off his dresser and dropped the magazine into his off hand. He then racked the slide to ensure that the chamber was empty before re-inserting the magazine and chambering a round of hollow point duty ammo. It was a practice that he did every time he touched a new weapon or took his pistol out at the end of the day. He had seen too many "professional shooters" negligently discharge their weapon, assuming it was unloaded. Even a couple cops.

Thor laid on his side and lifted his head lazily from his dog bed watching Glenn as he prepared for work, before stretching his long legs and falling asleep again, his brown muzzle and floppy ears nuzzled comfortably in the cushion of the bed.

By 6:30 AM Glenn was in his car and made his way to the Police Detective Division in downtown Tulsa, about a twenty-minute commute. As he drove, he couldn't help but think back to the last three weeks and all that had happened. His case was unusual to say the least and while he commuted, thought back to the first day when Scott had called him. His memory flashed back intermittently during the drive.

On the day of the incident, Glenn had driven to the Wabash trailer park and immediately saw firetrucks and police vehicles surrounding a smoldering trailer facing the south end of the park. Glenn maneuvered his vehicle behind one of the idling firetrucks and exited his vehicle. The scene was bustling with activity from first responders and inquisitive neighbors. A perimeter of crime scene tape the size of a football field encompassed the burned trailer and several surrounding trailers that had been damaged by the smoke and flames. Charred wood and ash littered the ground and firefighters were probing the rubble for sources of heat and flame. Metal siding and support beams lay amongst the heap of destroyed trailer. The smell of smoke was thick and heavy in the air.

Glenn approached the scene and ducked under the tape; a young Tulsa police officer came charging up to him, a sense of authority written on his face.

"Sir!" the officer said officially. "Sir you cannot be here, everyone must stay back. This is a crime scene!"

Glenn parted his suit jacket and revealed the detective's badge and Glock 17 on his right hip. "Would you rather work the scene instead? It would save me a hell of a lot of paperwork," Glenn answered. "Oh. Oh, I'm sorry detective," the young officer stammered; his confidence being pulled out like a rug from under him. "I didn't know."

Glenn chuckled. "That's right rookie, I go where I please. I appreciate you trying to keep the scene secure though. I'm Detective Blackthorne, Tulsa PD. Where is Detective Shoemaker?"

The rookie officer smiled and pointed towards a mountain of metal siding and melted plastic where the trailer used to sit.

"Last I saw, he was on the other side of all that shit, Sir."

Glenn thanked the officer and proceeded to Detective Shoemaker's last known location. Glenn walked behind the pile of rubble and saw his friend Scott crouching and inspecting what appeared to be a burnt glass dining plate. Scott looked up and greeted Glenn.

Scott rose and stood to his feet. Glenn was tall and lean, but he wasn't a patch on his friend. Scott was a head taller than him and at least thirty pounds heavier; all lean muscle. The pair were voracious gym rats and would constantly challenge each other in feats of strength and endurance. Glenn had speed, but Scott had power. Scott was a former Marine whose great pride was serving in the Marine Security Guard Detail in the White House some years back. When he left the Marine Corps, he had offers for high paying security contracts across the world. He instead decided that he was away from his wife for too long and needed to show the same devotion to her that he did to his work as a Marine. They moved back to Tulsa, and within six months, Scott Shoemaker was in the police academy.

"Well, this is a shit show," said Glenn.

"You're telling me," Scott responded. "And to make matters worse..." he motioned to the firefighters that were now rolling up their hoses. "The goddamn Evidence Eradication Team sprayed water all over the place and trampled through the entire scene."

Glenn looked at the firemen and back to Scott. "Well, Scott, the general public usually disapproves of firemen letting structures burn while they just stand around with their thumbs in their asses. The hose draggers have their job, we have ours. Where's the body?"

Scott winced when Glenn mentioned the body. "She was cooked. The body was relatively easy to locate, not much digging was needed. We could see what's left of her head and skull protruding from the ashes. She's been taken to the morgue and obviously we are gonna have to go by dental records. I got some photos if you want to see."

Glenn didn't have to imagine. He had been on several arson investigations in the past and had seen how the flames horribly disfigured their victims. In cases where the victim had burned to death, the brains began to boil inside of the skull and burst open when the pressure became too much for the skull to bear. It was an ugly sight.

"No, I'm good for now," Glenn said as he looked at the rubble. "You said SHE was cooked. How could you tell that the victim was a she?"

Scott shrugged. "I'm just guessing at this point. Dispatch's records say that Kelly Snow was the last known person to live here, but I can't tell you if this is her or not. Could be some meth-head who snuck in, smoked his shit, and burnt the place around him. Could be a different person. All I know is, is that the fire burned hot and fast because according to the neighbors, it went up in seconds, so I'm guessing it wasn't an accident and some sort of accelerant was used. Not that we'll ever find out, cause the goddamn kitten savers demolished any trace evidence, and I can't find the point of origin. I mean, you would think that they…" his voice trailed off.

"Think that they what?" said Glenn, turning back to look at Scott. Scott's face was gaunt and had turned ghostly white. He was staring at the debris pile and slowly started walking towards it.

"Scotty!" Glenn called. "Where are you going?"

Scott continued to walk toward the pile as if he were in a trance. Once he reached the edge, he kneeled, and with his bare hands, began to dig and move burnt wood out of his way. Glenn quickly walked over to him.

"Scott?" he asked softly.

Scott continued to move rubble away. Glenn had no idea what he was doing but was concerned for his friend. He squatted and was about to assist but then Scott stopped abruptly. His eyes were fixed on a charred piece of wood that was in front of them. "Damn it, Scott, what the hell are you doing?" Glenn demanded.

Almost inaudibly, Scott said, "I didn't know they were there."

"What?" Glenn asked, confused.

Scott pointed to the burnt wood. Glenn looked back at the wood and didn't comprehend what his colleague was trying to tell him. Trying to understand, Glenn traced the wood with his eyes. It was small and blackened;

approximately a foot long and at the end there appeared to be some melted plastic or rubber or....

Glenn shot to his feet. A horrible realization wormed through his body like lightning and although he was an experienced police officer, he was nauseated at what lay in front of him.

## FOUR

Glenn parked his vehicle in the parking lot of the Detective's Division and proceeded inside. Even at 7:00 AM, the office was bustling with phone calls and conversations. The office area smelled of old coffee and of freshly printed paper. Phones were ringing and the hum and flow of the office reminded him of ants in a nest. As he walked, Glenn noticed that he was receiving some uneasy glances as he neared his coworkers. When he returned looks at them, they quickly carried on their business. The arson case was…complicated, and there were mixed emotions with how it all played out.

He made his way to his tiny office and sat down and fired up his computer. A small mountain of paperwork decorated his desk and at times he wondered how he would keep up with it all. He began to check his emails and re-read the message from the Tulsa News Channel reporter, Kimmy Lee.

*"Detective Blackthorne,*

*Thank you again for agreeing to me with me for an interview. While I am sure that this case had significant emotional repercussions for you, I am sure that you would agree that the people of Tulsa deserve to hear the full story, especially since it involved trusted members of its police force. I am available to meet you at your office around 2:00*

*PM this Friday and conduct the interview. Please let me know if this works for you.*

*Regards,*

*K.L.*

*Tulsa News Channel"*

She had sent the message on Tuesday, but Glenn had never responded. *Maybe she won't come,* he hoped.

"Well, if it isn't the man of the hour!"

Glenn looked up from his computer. Standing in the doorway was one of Detective's Division's record clerks, Denise Young.

"Hi, Denise," smiled Glenn.

He had always liked her. She was a short, spritely woman of forty, with thick brown hair and a wire rimmed-glasses. She was very professional and very understanding.

Glenn truly believed that she was physically incapable of hurting anyone's feelings, which was amusing, because she worked in an office full of the foulest mouths this side of a Naval shipyard.

"Big day today!" said Denise. "You have the interview with Kimmy Lee! I always thought she was so pretty and not just another talking head. Will a camera crew be there too?"

"I don't know," Glenn replied. "I don't even know if she is coming today because I didn't respond to her email."

Denise could hardly contain her excitement. "I know, she called the office when you were away, and I confirmed the interview time for you! I hope you're not mad, I'm just so proud of you for being one of the good ones."

Glenn groaned. "A part of me was wishing that she wouldn't show up." Denise looked away, embarrassed.

"I'm sorry Glenn, I was just trying to help."

Quickly realizing his mistake, Glenn corrected himself.

"No, no, no Denise, you did nothing wrong, and I appreciate everything you do. I just don't want to talk about it. Scott…fucked up. I can already feel the heat rising in the office and I don't want this to add fuel to the fire." The irony of this last statement was not lost on him. "Besides, the Chief is wanting me to do this interview as well, so you saved me from an ass chewing."

Glenn's desk phone rang. He looked at Denise who smiled at him and left the office. Glenn answered the phone.

"Detective Blackthorne, homicide."

A woman's frantic voice answered. "Yes, hi, my name is Melanie Crix and I was told you could help me? I called 911 and they sent me to you."

*God damn it,* Glenn thought. *I told that fucking rookie down there to not be giving out my number to random callers.*

Glenn checked his frustration before answering.

"What exactly do you need help with Miss Crix?"

"It's about my sister, Isabelle," Melanie said. "She's been missing for two days now, and I am getting really scared. It's not like her to be gone this long and not call me. I've called our mom, and she hasn't seen or heard from her either. Her friends at work say that she hasn't shown up for work since Tuesday, and I don't know what else to do please, please, help me."

Glenn pulled out a notepad and pen from his jacket pocket. "Ma'am, I primarily work homicides, you should contact our Missing Persons Division. I can send your information over to-''

"I already tried that!" Melanie interrupted. "All I got was an answering machine and I am worried that time is running out and I know you work murders and stuff but what if she's already dead!" Melanie began to cry. "My sister is my only friend and I beg you to help me find her!"

Glenn sighed. Her situation was unfortunate, but resources were limited, especially since violent crime has steadily increased every year. The civilian population relied on the police to investigate and solve crime, but the police rely on funding from the city. With the modern economy recking havoc on fiscal capabilities, there were fewer and fewer police recruits each year. Starting salaries weren't as competitive as neighboring departments and that drove away potential candidates. Of those who did join, only a small percentage stayed on the job after seeing the constant gang violence, drug abuse, and overall depravity that humans were capable of. Once the veil of civility was removed, young officers were face to face with the true nature of the beast. Ludicrous call volumes and long hours further weakened their resolve and made them question why they ever joined. The dark underbelly of police work was revealed to them, and many couldn't hold the line.

"Are you sure she didn't take some time off or go on vacation or anything?" Glenn asked.

"I'm sure. She just bought a new Dalmatian puppy and it's still at our apartment, she loves that thing and would have taken it with her!"

Against his better judgement, Glenn succumbed. "Miss Crix, I will do what I can. Just be aware that I already have pending cases that also require my attention, but I will investigate your sister's disappearance. I am going to need some information from you first, though."

Denise poked her head into the room. Glenn held up a finger to tell her to wait but Denise mouthed *"Chief wants you to call him"* and left.

"First," he continued, looking back at his note pad. "When was the last time you saw your sister?"

Over the course of the following minutes, Glenn and Melanie asked and answered questions. He recorded the important details on his notepad and confirmed the information with Melanie. When satisfied, Glenn advised her that he would contact her as soon as he knew anything about Isabelle. He gave her his duty cell phone number and told her to call him if she could remember anything else or if additional information surfaced. He then hung up the call.

Glenn stood up and stretched his back. He picked up the desk phone and dialed the number for the Chief of the Tulsa Police Department. He knew that it was the big

Chief that wanted to talk to him, none of the other Chiefs would have granted him an interview based on the facts of the case.

"This is Chief Erickson," said a gruff voice on the other end. "Is this Blackthorne?"

"Yes sir," answered Glenn.

"Excellent, how are you doing today, Detective?" The Chief asked.

"Can't complain sir, just working my cases, caught another one just before I called you," Glenn said.

"Homicide?"

"Unsure yet, sounds more like a missing person right now."

"I'm sure you will get it handled," The chief said dismissively. "Anyway, I wanted to talk to you about this interview you are having today. I know it doesn't need to be said, but I'm going to say it anyway; do not embarrass this department any more than it has been."

Glenn felt like he got punched in the stomach. *How the hell was any of this my fault?* He gritted his teeth and fought the urge to say something he shouldn't.

"I didn't intend on being an embarrassment for the department, sir, however, I didn't do anything wrong either."

"Listen Blackthorne," said the Chief. "I've got City officials up my ass about this incident and to be honest, I didn't even want you to have this interview after our own internal investigation but, "the powers that be" have decided that it needs to be shared. I'm trying to control the bleeding the best I can, so I'm going to say this; don't give her too many details and don't give her any damn opinions."

"Roger that, sir." Blackthorne's way of telling someone to *"fuck themselves"* respectfully.

"Good man. Now, I know I said I wanted to meet you in person at one, but I think this little conversation will suffice. Blow Kimmy a kiss for me." Then the line went dead.

*That son of a bitch hung up on me!* Glenn thought angrily.

The minutes passed into hours and with each passing second, Glenn dreaded his interview with Kimmy Lee. The case was so emotionally charged, and it affected many different people in many ways, especially Glenn. There was no way of telling how this interview would go.

*Goddamn it, Scott. You really fucked me on this one.*

At 1:45 PM he needed a break. Glenn sighed as he drew himself from his desk. He had just enough time to step outside for some fresh air before the interview. He made his way to the East end of the building and went outside. He saw his longtime friend and fellow homicide Detective, Adrian "lemon" Meyer sitting on a bench and smoking a cigarette, watching the traffic flow by. Meyer and Glenn were in the same academy class together and Glenn was the one who gave him the nickname "lemon" on account of his name's resemblance to the fruit.

Detective Meyer noticed Glenn's approach and gave half a wave. "Howdy Glenn. Smoke?" His deep southern accent was marred and raspy from years of smoking.

"I don't smoke anymore, Lemon, you know that," Glenn replied.

"And YOU know that I have hated being called "lemon" all these years. Makes me sound like I don't work or I'm a dud or something."

"Well, you *DON'T* work. Look at you, old man, sitting outside while real cops are out busting their asses," Glenn retorted.

"If I'm not mistaken, you are outside with me!" laughed Lemon.

Playful banter is as important to police work as yeast is to bread. Cops make fun of each other to help build camaraderie and to decompress from the job. They often spent more hours with their co-workers than they did with their own families and the stress levels were liable to skyrocket very quickly. Banter and pranks were always there for them when the going got tough. Horrific scenes of death and unparalleled sadness were almost a daily occurrence. A much-needed laugh could take the edge off when it was needed most. Glenn could remember a time when he was a young officer and drove his patrol vehicle through a pothole that had loose chunks of concrete in it, which resulted in five thousand dollars' worth of damage.

He was reprimanded for the damage, and was down on himself, but the comedic minds at the station had printed out a reward poster with a picture of a rock on it saying, "Wanted for Criminal Mischief. Dead or Alive" and had left it on his desk; the gesture cheered him up instantly. The friendly jeering was also a sign of trust. *If we don't make fun of you, we don't like you.*

"I have my interview in a few minutes," Glenn said.

"So, I've heard," said Lemon taking another drag from his cigarette. "How ya feel about it?"

Glenn scratched his head. "To be honest, I really don't want to do it. There has been way too much bullshit circling over my head regarding this case and I just want to put it behind me."

"Fat chance," Lemon croaked. "This was a huge case, and you were the one who cracked it. So, use this as your chance to tell your side of the story. Forget all those other fucks upstairs, they didn't have to face what you did. Glenn, how do you navigate a minefield? One step at a time."

Glenn sighed. He knew he was right. Glenn was never one to let people's opinions get to him, especially when it came to his work. The fire, however, was different. Not only was it extremely taxing on his mental health, but it also withered his resolve. His once great mental fortitude had been nearly shattered by the events that had occurred, so now when he heard the rumors floating around the office, they got to him.

Glenn checked the time on his phone. "I gotta go Lem- *DETECTIVE* Meyer," he corrected.

Lemon chuckled. "Good luck Glenn. You'll be alright. I got your six on this one. Remember, if the glass is half empty…go fill it up!"

Glenn smiled and walked back towards the doors. That is one thing he loved about this job; some of the greatest people he had ever known were police officers. There was an unspoken understanding that it was a brotherhood; a group of men who go into danger together, who suffer together, and who win together. The covenant of the Thin Blue Line meant that I have your back and you have mine. In a world where assaults on officers are a constant threat, knowing that your comrades are watching over you is like having armor against those who would do you harm. Just like a family, an officer can count on their fellow officers to pick them up when they fall.

Glenn continued back to his office. He checked his phone again. There was a text message from a number he didn't have saved that only said, *Here.* Glenn assumed that someone had given Kimmy Lee his number and now she was impatiently waiting. He continued walking back to his office and tried coaching himself on some of the various questions she would most likely be asking. Some were easier than others. He knew that he would have to talk about Scott and his involvement in the arson case. He also knew that even if he laid out every event that happened to Kimmy, there would still be those who doubt the facts and want to draw their own conclusions.

Before entering his office again, Glenn stopped in the men's bathroom and threw cold water on his face and closed his eyes. The memories surrounding this case haunted him daily and he needed to be free of it. *The only way is forward,* he thought. *I will have to talk about my friend Scott Shoemaker. And how I killed him.*

# FIVE

She sat on the swing set at recess. Its rusty hinges squeaked and groaned with every movement. She scraped at the wood chips beneath her feet while she swung. The chains were in unison with the slow and methodical swings she commanded from it. She counted the fence posts across the playground, left to right, with laser focus. The bustle of children and the myriad of sounds throughout the playground was of little concern to her. Here, she was safe. Her own little world where she could not be bothered. She didn't have to be in fear on her swing. She didn't have to remember the man living in her home. The swing's loving embrace was her protector, and it was all she wanted. The hinges squeaked.

# SIX

The room was dark and musty. Standing in the doorway, the man watched the narrow stairs disappear into the inky murk. The hallway light behind him had no power against the impenetrable darkness that lay in front of him like a jet-black pool. He stared down into the abyss. A powerful odor wafted from the tomb like pit and caressed his nostrils.

*Soon,* he thought. *Soon we will have another.*

He always knew that there was some evil inside him, though its magnificence had not truly surfaced till he moved here. Now he could enjoy the fruits of his labor unhindered. He remembered his initial yearning for the kill, and the thought of his first made him squirm with delight.

*There will be others.* A noise emanated from the blackness. The sound of chains being dragged.

He smiled.

"Hello my brother."

# SEVEN

Kimmy Lee was in interview room two. The rooms were used by the detectives to interview suspects and victims. They were bleak and only had a single wood table and two chairs and a wall mounted video camera with a microphone for audio. The suspect was always given the chair furthest from the door, to create the illusion that they were trapped and had nowhere to go until they confessed. Kimmy Lee had graciously left that chair open for Glenn.

Before entering the interview room, Glenn went to the terminal that was out of sight of the interview rooms and ensured that the video and microphone were off and not recording. Satisfied as he could be, he walked to the room to greet his inquisitor.

"Hello Detective!"

Kimmy stood. She was an incredibly attractive woman with wavy black hair and a petite figure. Her distinct Asian features were subtly muted by the perfectly blended make up. Her smooth athletic legs extended out from under a sleeveless red dress and into black stilettos. The woman was the epitome of sex appeal.

Glenn cleared his throat and extended his hand. "Call me Glenn."

Kimmy returned the handshake. *Her hands are as smooth as silk,* Glenn thought, as he stared into her creamy brown eyes and for a second, forgot why he was even there.

Kimmy smiled. "Are you ready to begin?"

"Yes, yes," said Glenn, sitting down in his chair.

Kimmy sat and grabbed her purse from off the floor. She rummaged for a few seconds before removing a small black box the size of a sticky note. "It's my recorder. Helps me remember the conversation," Kimmy said. She placed the box between them in the middle of the table and pressed the red "Record" button. She looked back up and smiled at Glenn. "Can you please state your name and occupation?"

Glenn took a deep breath. *Here we go.*

"Detective Glenn Blackthorne, Homicide Division, Tulsa Police Department," Glenn stated.

"Thank you, Detective, first I would like to get to know you a little better, can you tell me how long you have been a police officer?"

"Just under fifteen years. Been a Detective for ten of them."

"Very impressive, what made you want to be a cop?" Kimmy asked.

Glenn paused. "Well, lots of things. I needed a good job with good pay that wasn't boring."

The answer was watered down. Glenn left the military and had absolutely no idea what to do with his life. He began drinking heavily and was quickly spiraling down the drain of self-doubt, anger, and depression. Sleep was difficult because he was constantly on guard and nearing paranoia. Memories of reality shattering battles replayed over and over in his mind. Seeing his fellow countrymen torn apart and crying for their families ripped a part of his soul away.

How could he ever explain to people what he saw or how he felt? The only ones that could understand is other soldiers, but there was a stigma about showing emotion with a group of young men who endured life altering events. You just have to endure it. Fake it till you make it. A popular saying the Army is *"embrace the suck"* meaning to accept your situation and carry on. Try as he might, Glenn felt hollow, like a ghost in purgatory that belonged neither with the living nor the dead. He occasionally wished that he had died with his brothers in combat. It would have been simpler. He often thought of a quote from Plato; *"Only the dead have seen the end of war."* After the military, Glenn had no direction. His life felt bleak and meaningless. The Army and war were all he knew.

*Maybe dad was right.*

While sitting in a crummy one-bedroom apartment one evening, he was watching the popular tv show COPS and for once in what seemed like an eternity, Glenn felt hope. As he watched, he could feel his spirits lifting and he began racking his brain. He suddenly felt himself longing to be with the officers on the tv. Courage. Duty. Sacrifice. The defining traits of a police officer were the same traits that he valued and lived by when he was a soldier. "I can do that," he thought out loud. "I can definitely do that." He continued to watch the episode and while one of the officers attempted to detain a suspect, the suspect wriggled free, and began to run away. The officer immediately began pursuing the suspect on foot, simultaneously calling for assistance over the radio. "Oh, get him!" Glenn yelled at the tv, "Get that son of a bitch!" He had not felt this invigorated or excited in a long, long time.

The officer continued to chase the suspect through a backyard and proceeded to jump over two fences before eventually tackling the exhausted suspect to the ground and placed him in handcuffs.

*This is the kick in the ass I needed.*

Glenn looked down at his stomach protruding from the bottom of his shirt. He had gained a few pounds since not having to participate in the intense physical training that occurred every morning in the Army.

"Alright," he said confidently. "I know what I gotta do."

The next morning, Glenn poured all of his remaining alcohol down the kitchen sink and crushed all of his cigarettes till they were nearly dust. *If I am going to do this, I need to stay disciplined,* he thought. *No excuses, no fooling around.*

Over the course of three months, Glenn forged his body into a strong, athletic tool. Not only did the weight come off, but also something else that he did not expect to leave. The human body is an incredible machine and while he trained and pushed himself, the depression withered away. He began to sleep better, his mood and mental clarity improved, and his confidence soared. He felt the same way he did while he was in the military. Strong and focused and willing to take on anything. His great reset had finally begun.

Kimmy was a professional and knew when someone didn't divulge all their information.

"Come on," she teased. "That can't be all?"

Glenn smiled. "I liked watching COPS on tv."

They both laughed and Glenn felt himself starting to relax. *Maybe this wouldn't be so bad after all.*

As if smelling blood in the water, Kimmy struck. "Tell me about Scott Shoemaker?"

Glenn hardened as quickly as he relaxed. He wasn't expecting to be talking about Scott so soon into the interview. A true chill went up his spine and, for a moment, he was speechless.

"Scott and I were good friends," Glenn began. "He was on patrol for a couple of years before I got on. We both worked the neighborhoods by the airport. Rough area. It was enough to keep us both busy."

"Did you enjoy working with him?" asked Kimmy.

"Of course," said Glenn. "At first, he was my FTO. An FTO is a Field Training Officer, they are the ones who ride around with the rookies and-"

"I know what an FTO is," smiled Kimmy. "They teach new officers and help keep them out of trouble."

"That's right," said Glenn. "Anyway, Scott pushed me to be more than "just a beat cop". A few years later, I applied to go to investigations, and he put his application in as well. Strangely, I got picked up before he did. After that, he and I worked homicide together till…" Glenn winced.

"The fire. His family and mine were close. We were like brothers."

"Well, I am glad you brought that up Detective, after all, that's the who reason why I am here," Kimmy said. "I am trying to get the full scoop with all the sprinkles. Too many rumors and unsubstantiated claims have circled this incident and I want to hear it from the source. What happened with the fire?"

Glenn sighed. *Here it is.*

"When I arrived on scene, Scott was already there. He said that he had taken photographs of the victim, but it was undetermined who the victim was because of the extent of the burns. The body was sent off to the pathologist's office to be examined and identified. While we spoke, Scott stopped mid-sentence and became very quiet and looked shocked, like a great realization came over him. He went the pile of rubble and went searching as if he lost something over there. I came over and joined him... and...uhm." Glenn had a difficult time acknowledging what he saw at the fire.

Kimmy was leaning forward, fully attentive to Glenn's every word. "Go on, Detective. What did you see?"

Glenn closed his eyes.

"A leg. A child's leg. It was burnt so badly that it looked like a piece of charred wood, but I saw the small plastic shoe that was on its foot, and I knew what it was. When we moved the rubble, we could also see that there was a second child. They were holding each other during the fire. It looked as if they hid from the flames together and... died together."

"Oh my God," Kimmy whispered. "That's awful!"

Glenn nodded in agreement. "The strangest part was that Scott seemed to already know. He even said that he "didn't know they were there" like he was aware of their existence. I chalked it up to him not knowing there were other victims and he just missed finding them. Things really got weird when the medical examiner called me and said that the adult victim was a female named Kelly Snow and she had traces of semen in her vagina. Scott was the lead investigator on this, and he said that he did not want the semen to be tested. When I protested, he got irate with me and pretty much told me to fuck off. I was on edge about the whole thing."

"So, what happened next?" Kimmy asked, hardly blinking.

"Well, Scott raised me in the world of policing. I trusted his judgement and figured that he knew what was best. The odds of us finding usable semen after being in a fire AND somehow finding who it belonged to was like finding a needle in a stack of needles. I just continued my investigation for a couple days until Scott called me one night at about 10 PM. He was hammered and slurring his words and I could hardly understand him. He told me he was at the Wabash trailer park and that I needed to go meet him there so he could explain everything to me."

Glenn's phone buzzed. He pulled it out of his pocket and saw a text from his mom:

*CALL ME.*

It vibrated again.

*Brrr brrr*

*URGENT.*

"I'm sorry, Kimmy, I need to make a quick call. Can we resume in a few minutes?" asked Glenn.

"Of course," said Kimmy. "I need a few minutes anyway to wrap my head around everything you've told me." She then hit the red button on her recorder to turn it off.

Glenn thanked her and stepped out of the room. He was thankful to have a temporary respite from the questioning and turned his thoughts toward his mom. His mother was a capable woman but tended to be overly dramatic at times. The last time he received an URGENT text from her, it was because the neighbor's cat was sitting on her porch, and she wanted him to help get rid of it. However, she was now nearing seventy years of age and lived alone so Glenn wanted to make sure that she was ok.

Glenn found a secluded area in the hallway and dialed his mom's number. It rang twice before she answered.

"Hello?" an old voice answered.

"Hi Mom. What's going on?"

His mother's voice sounded like it was about to break. "I'm sorry to call you while you're at work Glenn, but I thought you would want to know right away."

Glenn stiffened. His mother was very stoic and hearing her weepy voice made him uneasy.

"What happened?" He asked concerned. "Are you ok?"

With that, the woman's reserve failed her, and she began sobbing. "Oh, Glenn I'm so sorry. I know we all didn't get along, but it still hurts."

Glenn's mind raced. *What on Earth was she talking about?*

"MOM!" Glenn said sternly. "TELL ME WHAT IS GOING ON!"

"It's your father," she sniffled. "He's dead."

# EIGHT

Santina was walking home from school. It was Friday and the teachers wouldn't let her on the swings because no students were allowed on the property after hours. She didn't like going home, especially after seeing what she saw a couple days ago.

She turned the corner by the bent stop sign and walked another two blocks before seeing her house. It was small, way too small, and had faded yellow paint which began to chip. The wooden steps were worn and rotting to the point where the nails and screws wouldn't hold. They leaned to the right and groaned when she stepped on them.

The yard was littered with trash and old junk that momma had left there over the years. Among the hundreds of cigarette butts and empty beer cans, was a rusty washing machine and an old wheelbarrow decorating the yard, much to the dismay of the neighbors. They had even complained to the city and a code compliance officer came out once and gave momma a ticket. Naturally, momma made Santina pick it all up, but promptly began throwing her cigarettes and beer cans outside all over again. The one saving grace of the home's appearance was a single flower that grew through the crack of the concrete in the driveway. It was only a noxious weed, but Santina thought it was unique. Its long green vines and white flowers reminded her that no matter the location or circumstances, something beautiful can grow from it. She saw a commonality between her and the concrete flower. *One day*, she thought. *I will bloom too.*

Momma wasn't a good housekeeper, especially since Jackson moved in. Jackson was momma's newest boyfriend. He didn't have a job and stayed home all day, at least that's what Santina thought. Jackson had moved in about a year ago and he said he was from a small town in Texas. He was in his early forties and was tall and very strong and had lots of tattoos on his arms and legs. He was a handsome man, but he usually smelled really bad, like he didn't take baths or something. He religiously shaved his head and face and looked like the prison version of *Mr. Clean*. Jackson was also ruthless to her and momma, he yelled a lot and broke things. Sometimes he made momma's eyes purple.

Santina opened the front door and walked inside. Momma was sitting on their old brown couch smoking a cigarette and watching *Jeopardy!* She was wearing her uniform from the Kum and Go gas station down the street. She worked the evening shifts and Santina knew she had to go to work soon.

"Hi momma," Santina said.

"Shut up, Tina, can't you see I'm watching tv?" Only momma called her Tina.

"I'm sorry," Santina struggled. Her speech issues seemed to get worse when she was upset or scared. *Ill'mm sowwy*.

"I'm sowwy, I'm sowwy," her mother mocked. "You sound so fucking stupid when you open your hole. See, your daddy knew you were going to be trouble and that's why he left us. I should have just given you away when you were a baby. Would have saved me the headache of listening to your dumbass talk."

Momma wasn't always this way. Somedays she could be nice- at least- *nicer*. Santina once heard her mother on the phone saying that she had *BYE POLL ARE* disorder or something. She knew not to take it so personally, but it was hard, she wanted a loving relationship with the one person who should love her above all others. Not only was she alone at school, but she was also alone at home too.

"Ok momma, I'll try better."

*Maybe if I can talk better, she will be nicer?* she thought.

"Jackson is out with his friends right now. I have to go in early. Feed yourself and don't bother him," Momma said.

"Yes, momma."

Santina walked down the hallway towards her room. She passed the one bathroom in the house that everyone shared, and she also passed the door to the cellar. Santina wasn't allowed to go down to the cellar ever since Jackson moved in. He said it was his private space for when he needed to relax, Santina didn't agree but Jackson scared her, so she did as she was told.

She went to her room and closed the door. She looked at herself in her tiny hanging mirror and began to work on her speech.

"Hewwo, I'm Sannntina."

Unsatisfied, she tried again.

"Hewwo, Im Santiiina."

She was still unhappy about it. She then made sure to enunciate every letter.

"HELL OH," she said louder. "I'm Santina!"

*Getting better*, she thought.

"Hello Santina, I'm mom, shut the fuck up!" She heard her mother from down the hall.

Happier with today's progress, Santina decided that she was tired and wanted to take a nap. She took off her coat and her shoes and climbed into her bed. She lay awake for a few minutes, thinking about momma and school. She thought about the mean kids, Sally and Connor, but mostly she thought about Mr. Harrison. *He's a nice man,* she thought. *Maybe he can be my friend?* She eventually fell asleep and dreamt that she and Mr. Harrison had gone for a walk and had a picnic, and she didn't have any issues speaking and she wasn't at all embarrassed. Mr. Harrison was her best friend, and nothing would ever get between them.

She awoke to the sound of the front door opening and closing. *Momma must be leaving.* She rolled over and realized that her room was dark. She sat up and looked out of her bedroom window. It was dark outside; she had slept through the evening. She heard heavy boots walking slowly down the hall.

*Clomp, Clomp, Clomp.*

Santina quickly laid back down and closed her eyes, pretending to be asleep. The light from the hallway was shining under her door and she peered at it with half open eyes.

*Clomp, Clomp.*

A shadow appeared under the door, blocking the light from entering her room. Slowly her door opened. A figure stood in the doorway, the light was to its back, and its frame was silhouetted and undistinguishable, but Santina knew.

*It's Jackson!*

Santina shut her eyes and pretended to be fast asleep. She hoped that if he thought she was asleep, he would go away. With her eyes closed, she had to use her other senses to tell her what was happening. Jackson never moved. He just stood there and watched. She could feel his eyes burning holes into her as she slept. She could hear his heavy breathing. She felt so uneasy whenever he was around. His demeanor was sinister and rotten.

The door closed. She dared to open her eyes and saw that he was no longer in her room. The shadow from underneath her door was gone, and she heard his footsteps going back down the hallway.

*Clomp, clomp, clomp.*

A rustle of keys came next, and she heard them enter a lock. The lock on the cellar door. The door opened and closed, and she listened as his footsteps vanished down the stairs.

Santina took a deep breath. She did not like Jackson at all. She rolled over onto her back and stared at the ceiling.

*I wish he never came here.*

She thought about how mean he was to momma and how she could hear their arguments from her room, arguments that quickly turned physical. She thought about one fight she heard three nights ago. One of momma's friends from work had come over and her, Jackson, and momma were drinking. Santina couldn't remember how, but an argument started between the three of them. She heard a loud *thud,* and something hit the floor, hard. Santina opened her bedroom door as quietly as she could so she could see what was going on. Momma's friend was lying on the floor, bleeding from a wound on her head. Jackson was standing over her with a baseball bat in his hands.

"That'll show you, bitch," Jackson grunted.

Momma's eyes were wide with shock and her hands covered her mouth. "Jackson! Why did you do that! All she wanted to do was leave!"

"You know why, Tamara," said Jackson. "You promised to help me and that's why you invited her here," He then pointed towards Santina's room. "And so, help me God, I'll kill you and that fucking kid of yours too, if you try and back out now!"

Terrified, Santina closed her door too quickly and it audibly closed shut.

"What was that?!" Yelled Jackson.

Santina's heart pounded as she heard him coming down the hall. He burst through the door and grabbed her by the arm. She screamed in pain, and he shook her till she stopped.

"What did you see!" He demanded.

"Noffing! I ssswear!" She cried.

"Don't you fucking lie to me, you little bitch!" He grabbed her by the throat and shoved her against the wall. His strong hands were crushing her trachea and she struggled to breathe.

"Leave her alone!" Tamara screamed and tried to pull Jackson off her. Jackson reared back and punched her hard in the face and she fell onto the floor, motionless.

"Listen to me!" Jackson growled in Santina's ear. "If you tell anyone what you heard or saw, I will make sure you can't ever see anything again. I will tear out your eyes and feed them to you! Do you understand!"

"YES!" Santina cried. She would say anything to get him to let her go.

"Not a word!" Jackson repeated.

Santina nodded, tears streaming down her cheeks. Jackson let go of her and she slumped to the floor, crying and grasping at her throat. Momma began to stir and wake up. Jackson then walked out of her room and into the living room. Santina could hear him dragging something heavy. She didn't dare to look out her door this time. "Santina, go play outside," Jackson ordered. "Use the back door. Don't come back for a while and make sure you don't say a fucking thing to anyone."

It was almost dark, but she didn't care. Santina flew through the back door as fast as she could and ran to the school. She sat on her swing and cried. She had never been so scared in her life. Her throat hurt horribly, and she was worried about momma. *I can't say anything,* she thought. *He'll kill us.*

Santina blinked herself back to the present. She was staring at the ceiling again. She didn't know how long she had laid there thinking about Jackson and momma, but it must have been a while because her eyes were now dry. She rubbed them with the back of her hands and closed her eyes. She couldn't hear Jackson and she was thankful. She hated him. She hated him for touching her and hurting momma. She hated being afraid of him and he needed to go. The memory of what happened just a few days earlier was always circulating her thoughts and she knew she would never be rid of it. Not until Jackson was gone.

# NINE

Glenn stood still in silence. "Glenn? Glenn are you still there?" his mother called.

"Yes, Mom, I'm here," Glenn responded. "How do you know he died? Who told you?" Glenn's parents had been separated for nearly eighteen years.

"The Miami-Dade Police Department called me. Apparently, your father has kept me as his emergency contact all this time," his mother said almost fondly. "He was in a boating accident. He was swimming with his newest girlfriend and another boat ran over them. She survived but he didn't make it."

Glenn knew his father had a weak spot for younger attractive women and he knew that they also gravitated to him for his money. His mother told him that his father had retired and lived in Florida for the last six years.

"Christ," Glenn said. "That's a helluva way to go."

"Do NOT use the Lord's name in vain!" His mother scolded. She was a devout Catholic and didn't approve of her son blaspheming.

"Sorry. When are we planning a funeral?"

"I don't know," she said. "After all, he's not been my husband for a long time. I just wanted you to know that he passed. For what it's worth, I did love the man once. And I'm glad that I married him because it brought me you. Other than that, your father was an insufferable prick."

Glenn couldn't help but agree. He and his father were not on good terms and his father had a gift for pushing people away.

"Anyway, I love you. Call me later if you want to talk. We can discuss what we are going to do. Bye honey," His mom said.

"Bye mom," Glenn said and then hung up. Glenn pocketed his phone and walked back to the interview room.

"I'm sorry Kimmy but I have to go."

Kimmy looked up at Glenn who was standing in the door of the interview room. "Everything ok?" She asked.

Glenn nodded and told her about the call he had just received. They agreed to meet at a later date to conclude the interview. Glenn left the room and stopped by Denise's desk to tell her that he was going to be out for the rest of the day and if anyone needed him, they could call. He left the building and walked to the parking lot.

*I haven't spoken to him in what… sixteen years? Roughly?*

Glenn found his vehicle and entered it. He sat in the driver's seat and gripped the steering wheel tightly. "One God damn thing after another," he muttered before starting the vehicle and heading for home. On his way, he called Mary and told her he was coming home.

"Did something happen? Are you alright?" Her voice was concerned.

"Yeah, I'll tell you about it when I get home," he said.

"Okay," said Mary. "Did you do your interview?"

"Yes. Well, at least some of it. We can talk more when I get home. Love you," Glenn said dismissively.

"I love you too."

Glenn continued to drive home. As he drove, the radio was off, and he was lost in his thoughts. He had not spoken to his father in sixteen years, but it was still such a strange feeling to know that he was dead now. So many events had passed that he wished he could have told his dad about. Glenn noticed he was feeling sorry for himself and tightened up.

*No,* he thought. *He could have reached out to me too.*

Glenn's anger towards his father had long festered throughout his childhood and into his adult years. Enduring how he and his mother were treated and ridiculed brought with it long term resentment.

His father, Dr. James Blackthorne M.D., had always had a very high opinion of himself, like most Doctors do, well, at least, according to Glenn. Dr. Blackthorne was a prominent Oncologist at the Saint John Lafortune Cancer Center in Tulsa. When Glenn first dropped out of college and enlisted in the Army, he invited his father to meet him at a local coffee shop in an attempt to explain his change of heart; a mistake he wished he never made. Dr. Blackthorne agreed, and they decided to meet at 10:00 AM on that Saturday. Glenn, anxious about the conversation, arrived at the café twenty minutes early, but was surprised to see that his father was already there, sitting at a table with a drink in his hand, reading a newspaper.

Glenn stood in the entrance and watched his father for a moment and could not help but admire the man. A graduate of Harvard Medical School and senior Oncologist at his current hospital, his father was formidable and brilliant. Always impeccably dressed, with a well-groomed beard and thick salt and pepper hair that was slicked back, Dr. Blackthorne's presence commanded respect. Even at the age of sixty, his muscular frame bore an elegant Midnight Blue Brioni suit, and his left wrist adorned a ten-thousand-dollar Diamond Gold Rolex. His feet were clad in handcrafted Italian leather oxfords, and he drove a metallic gray Corvette that was meticulously cleaned and waxed. His father projected unrivaled confidence and success.

Often, Glenn thought he resembled a Mafioso more than a practitioner.

Hesitantly, Glenn walked over to the table and sat down. His father looked over top his reading glasses at him and began to fold the newspaper. Glenn was about to greet him when his father interrupted.

"So, you intend on killing and dying instead of doing something useful with your life?"

Any admiration Glenn was feeling had now evaporated; however, he had heard it all before. The endless rants. The emotional shaming. Manipulation. Unless Glenn was doing what his father expected of him, the man was cold. Dr. Blackthorne wanted his only son to follow in his footsteps and become a medical doctor. To him, they were the only people in the world who actually *made* a difference. According to Dr. Blackthorne, if you didn't have status, you were not worth his time.

"No, I do not intend on dying," Glenn retorted. "But I need to do something more interesting and fulfilling than sitting in a classroom learning about subjects that do not intrigue me. Plus, I have signed up to become a medic. So, we are both in the medical field, like you always wanted."

Dr. Blackthorne scoffed. "A medic? Do you believe that some run of the mill Army medic is actually comparable to a medical doctor? Or truly be considered health care? You are as close to a medical professional as a child in art class is to being Van Gogh."

*He always knows how to make me feel like I am an inch tall,* Glenn thought.

"I am a doctor," he continued. "I matter. I have status and fulfilment in my work, and it has become my identity. I am medicine and medicine *is* me. My clients and peers respect me because I hold myself to the highest standards of education and performance. Becoming a soldier is beneath you and you must reconsider what legacy you want to leave behind. I also make two hundred and fifty thousand dollars per year, I might add." He paused. "What is your starting pay as a soldier?"

"About twenty- four thousand a year," Glenn said.

"Oh good," frowned Dr. Blackthorne. "Just enough for you to buy a bottle of whiskey and a pistol and handle your PTSD the old-fashioned way."

The comment infuriated Glenn and could no longer control his temper.

"What the fuck is your problem?" He blurted. Years of repressed anger towards his father were now bubbling to the surface and he wasn't going to back down this time.

"Why do you always have to be an asshole! So, WHAT if I don't conform to your mold? Mom didn't want to either and that's why she left you, and why your wife before her did too! I don't want what you want, and if becoming a doctor will make me anything like you, then to hell with it. I don't need your permission or your blessing, and guess what's different about me now than when I was sixteen? I have my own car and credit card, so I am out of here. I wanted to have a civil conversation with you, but you are too narcissistic and egotistical to be civil. Fuck you and your demeaning bullshit."

Dr. Blackthorne despised profanity. He considered it too "blue collar" for an educated man. He began to protest but stopped when Glenn stood from the table and thrust his forefinger into his father's face and other patrons in the café turned to see what the commotion was. Glenn's tall, athletic frame was a menacing sight, especially when he was angry. His eyes were filled with fire, a flame of years of emotional abuse and self- doubt, that soon was about to become an inferno.

"Soldiers have fought and died so that you can spew that ignorant shit from your mouth. They also have more guts and honor than you ever will. What they lack in education they more than make up for in courage and hard work. You ever disrespect them in front of me again, we are gonna have ourselves a good old- fashioned fist fight," Glenn growled. "Do not confuse your "status" with my ability to kick your ass."

Dr. Blackthorne's eyes grew wide and shimmered with fear. It was apparent that he was not accustomed to being spoken to in such a manner. "I'm sorry, Glenn," he stammered. "Sit down, I want to share something with you." Reluctantly, Glenn sat down again. He loved his father, but he did not like him. There was a time when he idolized him but as he grew older, he saw more and more behind his father's façade and began to realize it was all hubris. Glenn adjusted his seat and gave his father an unamused look that said, *let's get this over with.*

His father was able to read the expression like a flashing neon sign and proceeded to pull out his wallet from his back pocket. He then removed a twenty-dollar bill and laid it on the table. He then searched one of his front pockets and fished out a handful of change, rummaged through the collection, and placed a penny on the table. He then returned the remaining change back into his pocket. Next, he oriented the penny and the twenty so that they were side by side in the middle of the table.

"I'm going to tell you something that your granddad once told me when I was deciding my path in life," Dr. Blackthorne began. "If you had these two in your pocket, and you lost the penny, would you care?"

Glenn thought for a second. *Where is he going with this?* he wondered.

"No, I reckon not."

"What about the twenty? If you lost it, would you care? Would you go look for it?"

"Well, yes," Glenn answered, still wondering what point his father was trying to make.

Dr. Blackthorne smirked. "Of course, you would. It has value, significantly more value than the penny does." Glenn was beginning to understand what his father was implying.

"A doctor is a twenty," Dr. Blackthorne continued. "A soldier is a penny. The government, the civilian populace, and even first grade children across the world know that a doctor is a valuable resource that helps advance the human race to new levels. Expert training and education have allowed us to become some, if not the most, respected professions on the planet. On the other hand, a soldier is a penny. Expendable. The military gives you just enough training and brainwashing so that you will follow orders and kill and die without hesitation. Militaries from all antiquity have a history of sending young men to die by the thousands to pursue political aspirations, whether they be justified or not. To them, you are just pennies. If you are lost, so be it. There will always be more pennies."

Glenn was silent. His father's words crashed into him like a title wave, and he was left floundering in its aftermath. His father did have a point though. Just by watching the news and reading books he could understand that soldiers were used as political pawns to do the bidding of their governments. However, there was still some resistance in the deep recesses of Glenn's conscience.

"I understand what you are trying to tell me," Glenn finally said. "But keep in mind dad, value is not only determined by your education and status. Ancient samurai valued honor and skill more than any other property. Spartans valued courage and prowess in battle over anything else. To me, value is a willingness to go into a dangerous unknown world and spend it with brave young men who also see the value in being part something greater than themselves. I know that we will never agree completely on this, but you need to respect my decision. I need to serve my country and not take my freedoms for granted like so many Americans do."

It was Dr. Blackthorne's turn to get angry. "I had already accepted you making the frivolous choice of attending business school and look how that turned out. And where is the honor in getting killed or getting mangled? Or what about losing your soul from killing someone? Why don't you ask the dead if honor mattered, see what your answer is."

Glenn glared into his father's eyes. "Where's the honor in being a coward."

"Your youthful ignorance is showing, Glenn, and if you were half as smart as you think you are, you would see it." Dr. Blackthorne shook his head and said sternly, "Someday son, someday you will understand, when you have a family and children of your own." He leaned across the table, and with his eyebrows furrowed and with a scowl of his own said, "You will understand how hard it is to watch your children fuck up."

    Glenn stood from the table without a word and left the café. It was the last time they ever spoke. To this day, Glenn was occasionally reminded of their last interaction and how his father's words had stung him. Glenn never knew why his father couldn't see a world outside of his own and understand that value and status comes in many different forms.

    Glenn drove home from the office in a trance. He felt a deep sense of regret that he had not spoken to his father in all this time. Maybe they could have reconciled some of their differences now that he was an adult. Glenn secretly had always wanted his father's approval after their meeting at the café. Subconsciously, he wanted his father to know he was successful in his own way and maybe change their relationship. He wanted to share his experiences from the Army and his marriage and his life as a police officer. He wanted to prove to him that he wasn't the failure his father predicted him to be.

*It's too late now*, he thought.

He returned home and was greeted by Mary who was sitting on the couch. Mary worked remotely as a medical coding and billing agent, which allowed her to stay home, which Glenn liked. She glanced towards him and signaled that she was on the phone and would be finished shortly. Glenn hung up his keys and walked to their bedroom. He changed out of his suit and put on a Tulsa Drillers T-Shirt and gray sweatpants before walking back to the kitchen. He could hear Mary on the phone and typing furiously away on her laptop.

Glenn opened a cupboard above the stove and removed a bottle of Dalmore 15-year Scotch and clean glass. He sat down at the table and poured the glass half full before lifting it to his lips and draining it. The sweet, aromatic liquor went down with a delicious burn and in seconds he could feel a warming sensation coursing through his body.

He began to pour himself another glass but noticed that he didn't hear Mary typing anymore. He looked around and saw her leaning against the doorway of the kitchen.

"That kind of day, huh?" she asked, already knowing the answer.

Glenn nodded and poured another drink. "Yep. That kind of day. That kind of month. Actually, it's been that kind of year!"

Mary sat down at the table. They had just sat at the table this morning together and it already felt so long ago.

Glenn finished his second glass. "Today has been shit, my love, truly. The whole day has been shit." He could feel the alcohol loosening up his tongue and Glenn's brain-to-mouth filter was no longer in place. "Not only can't I sleep, but I am also bombarded with bullshit all day. I caught another case when I shouldn't have, the Chief was a prick, the office hates me, the interview sucked, and I found out that my fucking dad just died," Glenn grunted as he poured another glass.

Mary had been married to Glenn long enough to know that when he was in this kind of mood, to try and not take it personally.

"Wait, your dad died? How?" She asked.

Glenn drank half of his drink and coughed. "He got run over by a boat somewhere in the ocean. He was swimming with some skank, and the other boat didn't see them, and *SHHWIIP*." Glenn shot his hand across the table demonstrating what happened. "Went right over them. The chick lived but dad died. My mom called me about a half hour ago and told me."

Mary eyed Glenn closely as he tried to pour another drink, spilling some on the table. Almost half of the bottle was gone already.

"Oh my God, that is horrible! Are you doing ok?" Mary asked.

Glenn held up his glass of whisky. "Does it look like I'm doing ok?" He then drank it, sputtering and spilling some on his shirt.

Mary had was concerned with how quickly her husband was getting drunk. Especially since he seemed to be in a fantastic mood.

"I never met your father. He didn't even come to our wedding," Mary said sadly.

"That's because I never invited him. Trust me Mary, the guy was an asshole. You wouldn't have liked him, and he wouldn't have liked you." Glenn was beginning to noticeably slur his words. He then tried to pour himself another drink.

"Maybe you've had enough," Mary said cautiously while putting her hand on the bottle, stopping him from pouring. "You're already drunk."

Glenn looked at her and yanked the bottle free, grunting angrily.

"Is that right? You'd make a great Detective Mary, but you'd have to get off your ass and leave the house first."

Glenn was tip toeing on the line.

"Excuse me?" Mary said incredulously.

"Never mind," mumbled Glenn as he tried to pour another glass, spilling more this time.

"You're not going to talk to me like that Glenn Blackthorne, do you understand?" Mary scolded.

Glenn was silent. He swirled the whiskey in the glass and watched the amber colored liquid as it swished. He was angry at the world, not at Mary, but somehow, he couldn't keep his infamous temper under control, and she was a target of opportunity. His empty stomach processed the alcohol much quicker and made him more intoxicated by the second.

"Besides, alcohol isn't going to help your situation. It's only going to upset you more," Mary said, frustrated with Glenn's behavior.

"How do you know what will help me?" Snapped Glenn. "Do you know the kind of pressure I'm under? No. You sit at home with your cushy job and lack of responsibility."

Glenn was teetering on the line now.

"I've seen and done some shit that would give you nightmares for the rest of your life, Mary," he mocked. "How stressful is your job? Do you sometimes get a cramp from typing? Maybe get a rude email?" Glenn leaned closer to his wife. "Have you ever seen a dead body other than on the tv, Mary? Or what about an infant chopped into pieces and flushed down the toilet? Or what about watching a young woman jump off a bridge into traffic because she thought she had no other way out? Have you ever seen a rotting corpse or a raped child or fucking anything other than your computer screen?!" Glenn's face was flushed with anger.

"Glenn please calm down," Mary pleaded.

"No! I won't calm down!" Glenn roared, smashing his hand thunderously on the table. "You always think you know what's best for me! You haven't had to experience what I have. I had to KILL my best friend, Mary! He's dead! He's gone. Now this whiskey is my friend."

Tears were starting in Mary's deep blue eyes. "Glenn, I have always cared for you, you know that. I don't know why you are treating me this way, I was only trying to help." She began shaking in fear. She had never seen him this way before.

"You don't know anything, Mary," Glenn slurred.

Mary had enough. "I know that you are being an asshole! I have always loved you through the hard times and have always supported you. Just because you are suffering does not mean you get to take it out on me! Maybe it's a good thing I never met your dad, because it sounds like I'm living with another version of him!"

Glenn hiccupped. "Well good thing there won't be a baby Blackthorne, huh Mary. Won't have to deal with another version of me again."

Glenn had officially crossed the line.

Earlier that year Glenn and Mary were trying to conceive a child, but to no avail. After a visit to Mary's OBGYN, it was then learned that she was barren and unable to have children. The news devastated them both but was especially difficult for Mary. Glenn used it now as a weapon, a decision he truly regretted.

Mary stiffened. "What did you just say to me?" she asked icily.

Glenn began to back pedal, sensing his impending demise. "I shouldn't have said that. I'm sorry that-'' Mary cut him off. "Who the fuck do you think you are talking to me like that?!" Mary screamed. "How dare you say something like that to me! You have a bad day and get drunk and then treat me like shit, like I've never suffered or done anything for you?" She slapped him hard across the face, causing him to fall out of his chair.

Glenn sat up. "Mary, I'm sorry," he said as he rubbed his cheek. *She really got me good,* he thought. She had never hit him before.

"It's too late for that," Mary snarled, the tears flowing freely. "I asked you to calm down and you decided to be a jerk. You had your chance. Now you can sleep down here tonight with your new friend." She pointed to the bottle of whiskey on the table.

"Babe, I said I was sorry!" Glenn said as he reached for her hand. Mary snatched it away angrily. "Don't touch me, don't talk to me. I don't even know what else to say to you. It's incredible how you push those closest to you away."

Mary's words cut through Glenn's drunken haze.

*I'm acting just like dad.*

Mary spun quickly and ran to the bedroom, slamming the door shut. Glenn could hear her crying.

"Nice job, fuckface," Glenn muttered as he picked himself off the floor.

Glenn's shirt was soaked with the scotch from his glass. When she hit him, it spilled all over his chest and stomach as he fell to the floor.

He straightened the chair he sat in and grabbed a paper towel roll from under the sink and began to clean up the spilled liquor. As he cleaned, he no longer felt angry; he felt ashamed. Mary was the greatest person he ever knew, and he treated her like a punching bag. She only deserved the best version of him, and he thanked her for her unending love by acting like a selfish jackass.

He finished wiping the whiskey off the table and floor and stumbled outside to his back patio. The evening sun was making its descent across the sky and the air was warm and humid. He sat in a lawn chair and looked across his backyard.

*You're a goddamn fool for talking to her like that.*

Glenn's regret for his behavior only compounded the emotions that were bubbling around inside him. Scott was gone and it was his fault. He no longer enjoyed being a police officer. The joy he once had wearing the badge had faded ever since the fire. The intensity of the transpired events had stripped any love for the job he had left. To top things off, his dad passed away. A man he loved but also despised. The love and the hate for his father had also been a tug of war inside of him. He just wished his dad would have accepted him enough to bury the hatchet.

Glenn punched himself in the side of the head. *She's right you know. I don't know who you think you are, but you're NOT. Now because of you, your wife is crying in her room. You treated her just like how your dad treated you.*

Glenn punched himself again. *You're more like him than you realize.*

# TEN

It was Saturday again, and Santina Shard found herself on the swing, trying to forget the fear she felt the night before. When she closed her eyes, she could still feel Jackson's presence in the doorway and could hear his breathing. She tried forcing the memory away but was unable to. She felt her heart racing remembering what kind of a monster he truly was.

She opened her eyes and only saw fence posts. The squeaking hinges sang to her as she swung. The sun was bright and warm, but she still had her zebra striped coat on. The swing was her place to disappear and not be bothered.

Santina swung in her swing, counting the fence posts for hours. She didn't want to go home to Jackson and Momma. Anxiety crept its way into her brain every time she thought about going home. Jackson was up to something evil; she just knew it. There had to be a way to get him out of her and Momma's life.

Across the street, Glenn began waking up. He had dreamt that he was staring at a beautiful exotic bird and the bird was chirping constantly. When he opened his eyes, the bird disappeared but the chirping continued. He yawned and pulled the sticky sweat covered shirt off his body. His head was pounding, and the Oklahoma sun was a demonic fireball that was hell bent on blinding him. His mouth was dry, and his skin was sunburnt from passing out in the sun. He smacked his mouth to try and generate some moisture.

*Goddamn.*

He stood to his feet and stretched, his back and knees popping. He looked down at his watch to check the time. 11:00 AM.

*Finally caught up on some sleep.* He thought back to the day before and his fight with Mary.

*Shit. I thought that was a dream. Speaking of dreams, what is that chirping?*

It sounded like it was coming from the playground at the elementary school a block away. Glenn walked across his lawn and peered over the privacy fence at the school.

*Oh. It's her again.*

Glenn had seen that little girl before; the one who always wore the zebra coat. She constantly sat on the same swing set and would go back and forth for hours. Normally he tuned the noise out but today his hearing was acute, and every squeak was amplified by the hangover.

Glenn looked up and squinted against the sun. A dog barked in the distance. The squeaking was incessant, and it caused Glenn to grind his teeth. *A little peace and quiet would do nicely.* He walked back to his back door and stepped inside. It took a minute for his eyes to adjust to the dimly lit kitchen before he could make out any features. His head throbbed horribly, so he went and removed a glass from the cabinet and filled it with water from the sink. Glenn then opened another cabinet and took down a bottle of Tylenol and popped two into his hand. He then proceeded to chew the Tylenol and wash it down with the water.

He refilled his water glass and turned around to face the rest of the kitchen, when he noticed a note addressed to him sitting on the refrigerator. Approaching the note, Glenn began reading:

*Glenn,*

*I have gone to my parents for the rest of the weekend. I think some time away will be good for us. I'm sorry that things have been difficult for you, but you must remember that I am on your team and your actions yesterday were completely unacceptable. I am sorry that I hit you but after all… you did deserve it. You scared me and I don't care for how you made me feel. WE obviously have things to work on, but I want you to know that I love you and I will see you on Monday.*

*M.*

Glenn read the note again. He had forgotten how aggressive he had been towards his wife. It was a rare occurrence when he raised his voice at her but when he did, it was only detrimental to their marriage. Mary was very understanding that Glenn suffered from a mild form of post-traumatic stress disorder from his time in the military and as a police officer. She was even aware that Glenn had deep seated resentment towards his own father that would boil to the surface from time to time. What she would not tolerate, however, was Glenn acting like a fool and belittling her. Mary had come from a broken home where her father was a drunk and would scream at her and her sisters daily. Undoubtedly, Glenn's performance yesterday forced Mary to recall old fears and emotions.

    Glenn sat down at the kitchen table and finished his water. The Tylenol was taking its time to kick in and every second felt like an eternity. He checked his pocket for his cell phone and was relieved to see that he had no missed calls or messages. Though he was upset that he fought with his wife, Glenn was also looking forward to having the house to himself. He had not had any real alone time for a while and a reprieve from the chaos of his world was welcomed. The news about Mary's infertility was heart wrenching and it caused Glenn a great deal of pain, more than he ever let Mary see. The arson case and Scott's death were exacerbating Glenn's stress levels, and it was taking its toll. Having some time to himself was what the doctor ordered.

The Tylenol was finally beginning to take the edge off his headache and Glenn decided that he needed some more sleep. He walked back to his bedroom and closed the curtains shut. The room darkened instantly and felt like his own personal cave for his slumber. He crawled into bed and tried not to think about anything.

Glenn could see Scott standing in the rubble of the burnt trailer. It was dark and the porch lights from the surrounding homes bathed the area a dull orange. Scott turned to Glenn, a hopeless look in his eyes. Scott frowned and raised his right hand.

"Don't do it Scott! Glenn ordered while drawing his pistol. "Put it down!"

*BANG!*

Glenn awoke startled and with his heart feeling like it was bursting out of his chest. He was breathing heavily, and it took him a solid minute to remember that he was in his room.

*Nightmare.*

He put his head in his palms and watched as the dream faded from memory. He shook his head and rubbed his eyes and felt his pulse returning to normal. He took a deep breath and looked at the clock on his nightstand. 3:47 PM.

Glenn yawned and crawled out of bed, stretching as he stood. *I'm so tired of dreaming about Scott,* he thought. He checked his phone and saw a missed text message from his mom, asking if he was doing ok. Glenn wasn't in the mood to talk to his mother and set the phone on the nightstand. He sat back down on the edge of the bed and blinked to try and exit his stupor. As he sat, he could hear the "chirping" of the swing set.

"She's still out there?" he grumbled as he stood again. He turned on the lamp by his bed and proceeded to find his socks and an old pair of running shoes before donning them. He padded his way out into his immaculately cleaned living room and looked around. Aside from the squeaking, the house was eerily quiet, and he found himself thinking about Mary. He considered calling her but decided against it.

*She'll call when she's ready.*

Glenn decided to go for a run and clear his head. Exercise had always done wonders for his mental clarity. He stepped outside into the muggy sun and began to stretch. The feeling of the muscles lengthening and contracting were already improving his mood. He walked to the end of the block which intersected the main street that the elementary school resided on. Glenn saw the girl on the swing and wondered if she was ok. She had been out there for a while, and he wanted to make sure she didn't need anything. He proceeded to the sidewalk that went parallel to the swing set and approached the girl, whose back was to him. As he neared, it looked like she was counting something in the distance with her forefinger.

"Hello there!"

Surprised, Santina whipped her head to her left and saw a tall man approaching her. He was wearing a Tulsa Drillers T-shirt and an old pair of gray sweatpants. *Was he talking to me?* She thought. The man eventually made his way close enough to her that she could see his face. He stood on the sidewalk and leaned against the short chain link fence.

"How are you doing today?" He asked.

"I am not supposed to talk to strangers," she said stuttering shyly.

The man nodded approvingly. "That's a good rule. Did your parents teach you that?"

Santina was silent but continued to swing.

"That's ok," the man said. "I am actually a police officer. I was just checking to see if you were doing ok. I've seen you were out here alone for a while today, so I wanted to make sure everything was alright."

"I like to swing," Santina said. She inspected the man in normal clothing. "Where's your gun?" she asked cautiously.

The man laughed again. "I'm off duty today. Just going for a run and thought I'd check in with you. Are you doing alright? Do your parents know you are out here?"

Santina was silent again. She didn't want to think about home and hoped this man wouldn't make her leave and go back.

"Yes," she fumbled.

"Okay," said the man. "Well, if you ever need help, and your parents aren't around, I live just down the street there, 228 Carson Way. What's your name?

"Santina."

"What's that?" the man asked. "Can you repeat that?"

"Santina!" She said, proud that she didn't stutter.

The man smiled. "Nice to meet you Santina, I'm Glenn. I'll let you get back to your swinging. Take care." The man then walked off.

Santina continued to swing. She wasn't used to people treating her so nicely and this man didn't even bring up her stutter. He was a stranger, but Santina couldn't help but feel disarmed by his friendly demeanor and smile. She smiled shyly and watched him as he tied his shoes and began jogging out of sight.

*Cute kid,* Glenn thought as he began his run. He passed the bent stop sign and continued heading straight, following the sidewalk. As he ran, he could still hear the swing's hinges creak behind him.

# ELEVEN

## Amarillo-1995

"It's called Intermittent Explosive Disorder, Mrs. Trunt. Your son is suffering from an acute mental condition where he grossly expresses anger in a violent manner. Also,

I believe that due to Jackson stating that he sometimes hears voices that tell him to act out on his anger, he may also be suffering from Schizophrenia. It is still too early to tell, but we can start him on some medication and see if that improves his moods and outbursts."

Rebeca Trunt shifted in her chair. Her thirteen-year-old son, Jackson Trunt, was sitting next to her, scowling at the Psychiatrist. "Dr. Henshke, I don't know what else to do with him," she said. "His anger is getting out of control and do he honest with you…" She glanced at her son who now aimed his scowl at her. "He is beginning to scare me. I thought that him seeing you the past few weeks may have improved his demeanor, but he is still just the same, angry, kid. Both he and his brother act out at the slightest irritation." Mrs. Trunt began to sob as she spoke.

Dr. Henshke stood from his chair and walked around his desk towards Rebeca. He sat softly on the edge of the desk so that he could be closer to console the distraught mother. "It will be ok, Mrs. Trunt. I promise that I will do everything that I can do to help you and your boys. I have to say, the probability of both your sons developing the same mental conditions is… unusual, but with the right medication and therapy, I truly believe that we will be able to overcome this, and we can all move forward."

*This is one fucked up family,* the Doctor thought to himself. *Two children having IED and hearing voices? This is a first for me.*

Mrs. Trunt continued to sob. Jackson looked at her with disgust. He hated it when his mother cried and decided to break his silence.

"This is bullshit," he said. "Quit your blubbering, you fucking cow!"

"Jackson!" Rebeca Trunt cried. "You do not use that kind of language, especially towards your mother! See,

Doctor? This is what I am talking about! He is a powder keg and blows up over nothing! His brother Gabriel is the same way! Could it be because they are twins? Did I do something wrong when they were in the womb?"

Dr. Henshke shook his head. "Absolutely not. It is extremely rare that they both suffer from the same condition, but unfortunately medical science has not yet evolved far enough for us to know why some people develop certain conditions. What is known, however, is that teenage males have an underdeveloped frontal lobe which helps control emotion. The Medulla Oblongata with parts of the Limbic system can also affect temper and emotion. I recommend that the boys get plenty of exercise, plenty of sleep, and start a journal when they get angry so they can express it in a healthy manner."

Jackson stood and grabbed his own crotch. "I've got your frontal lobe right here!"

Jackson's mother was appalled by his behavior, but ignoring him, Dr. Henshke continued. "I want to see them both again. Separately of course. I don't want them feeding off each other's energy. I am available next week on Tuesday and Wednesday. After I see them again, you and I can discuss medications," he said as he put his hand on her shoulder. "We will get through this together."

"Doctor, did I ever tell you that I was actually supposed to deliver triplets? The other child…well…didn't make it, and my OBGYN told me that sometimes when a fetus dies inside… the other babies can actually absorb it. Is that true? Could that have some weird effect on their development as well?" Rebecca asked. Doctor Henshke nodded as he returned to his chair and sat down. "It's called Vanishing Twin Syndrome. It's where one or multiple fetus die during gestation and the host body reabsorbs it. In some cases, the other fetuses inside the womb absorb it as nutrients. It is a fascinating phenomenon. I actually wrote a paper on it in college, comparing the Vanishing Twin Syndrome and what they call, "the womb survivor" and the psychological effects they feel later on in life."

Dr. Henshke paused a moment. "Although each case is different, it is starting to make sense to me know why your sons have similar difficulties in life. Some symptoms of being womb survivors are feeling outcast and not knowing their true potential. It sounds to me like they have both absorbed some of the third fetus and both suffer from some of the mental side effects."

Doctor Henshke looked at his watch. "Well, that looks like that is all the time we have for today. You can schedule your next appointment with my assistant, Linda. I hope you guys have a good rest of your day. You too, Jackson." Rolling his eyes, Jackson stood to his feet and exited the room with his mother.

After the meeting, they drove home in silence and ten minutes in, Jackson spoke up. "I'm not taking any medication. There's nothing wrong with me. Maybe you should just stop pissing us off."

Mrs. Trunt sighed. "Jackson, I love you and your brother with all my heart, but this has to stop. I didn't even tell the Doctor about the threats that you two have made towards me because I didn't want you to be taken away."

*"She's lying to you,"* A demonic voice told Jackson. *"She doesn't love you."*

They continued home to their small house on the outskirts of Amarillo. Jackson looked out his window and saw it in the distance. It was a two-bedroom farmhouse that resided on thirty acres that once held some cattle and horses. Ever since Mr. Trunt died, the acreage was overgrown with weeds and all the other structures on the farm were rusting and deteriorating. Mrs. Trunt worked full-time for a truck dispatch center in Amarillo, and she had no time to tend the farm. Jackson and Gabrielle were homeschooled because they had both been expelled from previous schools for fighting and being aggressive with teachers and other staff; this lack of supervision at home allowed them to further continue their nefarious actions. Just last week, Jackson and Gabriel were caught trying to shoot a cow in a neighboring pasture with a shotgun they found under their mother's bed. The police had such a difficult time dealing with them, they just returned the delinquents back to their mother with a warning, much to the neighboring rancher's dismay. The Trunt boys were notorious hooligans that would throw a punch first and ask questions later.

As Jackson and his mother turned off the main highway and onto the county road towards their home, they saw a young man walking down in the ditch by the road. He was headed East, same as them, and he looked disheveled and worn. Mrs. Trunt slowed the car and rolled down Jackson's window.

"Hi mister. You need a ride?" She asked.

"That's awful kind of you ma'am, but the problem is, I ain't got nowhere to go," the man said in a thick Texas accent.

Jackson studied the drifter. He was tall and thin, like he had not eaten much in the last few weeks. The man looked to be in his early to mid-twenties and had a significant amount of stubble on his face. He wore a dirty white Stetson, and a ratty Carhart jacket. His jeans were stained from his travels and his boots appeared to have been used beyond repair. He wore a black backpack that was military in appearance. Even from inside the car, Jackson could smell that the man had not bathed or washed his clothes in some time.

"Well," Mrs. Trunt continued. "I can give you a ride to our place, it's just that white house up yonder," she pointed at the house through the windshield. "We got a phone you could use, and I can feed you supper. In the morning, I can take you where you need to go." Southern hospitality at its finest.

The man contemplated the offer. "That's awful kind ma'am, but I have nothing to offer in return for your kindness."

Mrs. Trunt eyed the man and winked. "I'm sure we can figure something out."

*"SLUT,"* The demon voice whispered.

With that, the man thanked her and opened the back door, set his backpack on the seat and climbed in. Instantly, the car reeked of unwashed clothing and body odor. Rebeca put the car in gear and started driving home again.

"I must apologize ma'am. I know I must smell something fierce," The man said. "I've been on my own for about a week now, I just got out of the Navy and have had nowhere to go. I was laid up in a hotel for the last two months but, embarrassingly, I spent all my money in Amarillo on gambling and liquor and put myself in quite the pickle. They kicked me out the hotel and here I am."

"Oh, bless your heart!" Mrs. Trunt said sympathetically.

"My name's Everett by the way. Everett Morrison."

Mrs. Trunt introduced herself. "I'm Rebeca Trunt. This is my son, Jackson. My other son Gabriel is at home. And don't worry, I've been down on my luck too. Sometimes all it takes is a little kindness to get back on your feet." She looked in the rearview mirror and smiled at him. Her pretty features and kind smile caused Everett to smile shyly in return. Jackson noticed the exchange.

"Are we really going to just let some stranger into the house?" Jackson asked. "You don't know this guy or anything about him."

"Jackson, mind your manners," his mother said sternly. "This man is in need, and we are going to help him. That's what good Christians do."

Sensing the tension, Everett spoke up. "I know it's awkward fella, but I assure you that I mean you and your family no trouble. I am just mighty appreciative that ya'll came by when ya did. I was starting to think I was coyote food."

Jackson spun quickly in his chair and glared at Everett. "Shut up faggot, I wasn't talking to you!"

"Jackson Trunt!" His mother scolded, "Have you completely lost your mind?! Apologize, immediately, young man! I do apologize, Mr. Morrison, my sons have some anger issues that we are working on. Please don't take it personally."

Confused, Everett responded. "Maybe it's not a good idea if I come home with you. I don't want to impose, and after all, he's right. You don't know me, and I don't want to upset ya'll any further."

"Oh nonsense," Mrs. Trunt replied. "It will be ok, you just come on to the house and we will get you settled in and…" She looked hard at Jackson. "It will blow over." Everett reluctantly agreed. He was tired of smelling like a dumpster and his stomach growled in protest of the extended fasting of food. The woman's kindness gave him a feeling of hope and gratitude and the thought of sleeping in a bed gave him great comfort.

They made small talk for the remainder of the drive. The car pulled up the dirt driveway and Jackson could see his twin brother throwing rocks at the feral cats that littered the property. Gabriel paused his entertainment for a moment when the car approached the house but resumed shortly after. Jackson quickly exited the car and headed over to his brother. Mrs. Trunt escorted Everett into the house, who was still profusely thanking her for her generosity.

Jackson approached his brother who had just landed a direct hit on a gray tabby that was unfortunate enough to be seen. Gabriel looked back at his brother and frowned. "Who's that?" he asked. Jackson rolled his eyes. "Some fucking stray the bitch decided to pick up and take home."

Gabriel glanced at the house and back to his brother. "That whore. Dad hasn't even been dead a whole year and she's already bringing other men home? He's rolling over in his grave. He gave her everything and she repays him by spreading her legs the first chance she gets."

Jackson looked at the house himself. "I hate her."

"Me too," said Gabriel.

Mr. Trunt had died while on duty as a volunteer fireman. Earlier that year, the area was plagued by grass fires due to the lack of rain and scorching temperatures. That particular fire's inception was caused by a couple of thugs cooking meth in an abandoned shack. Their inexperience led to the explosion of the lab, which scattered flaming debris across the field they were in. The bone-dry vegetation went up in seconds, and in addition to high wind, created an inferno that moved at a frightening pace. Eric Trunt's volunteer company was called out to assist. They had arrived on scene and were ordered to flank the fire to stop it from crossing the road to the west. The truck and engine were in position when there was a sudden wind shift and the fire burned over their position with no warning. The firemen attempted to back their vehicles out of the burn over, but in their haste, backed into a ditch where the fire and smoke soon overcame them. The news of the four dead and six wounded firemen sent shockwaves throughout the community.

    The Trunt boys were close to their father and his death left a void in their lives. They're already troubled thoughts grew darker and more sinister after their father had died. They had both begun to hear a "voice" inside their heads, a voice that would whisper to them in the deep recesses of their minds. Because Jackson and Gabriel were so close and this voice affected them both, they took to calling it, *The Third*. They believe it had something to do with there being another fetus inside their mother's womb while they were both gestating, but it died before birth, and somehow its spirit lingered on. The Trunt boys had a sickening feeling that it was their unborn brother speaking to them. At first, they rejected its presence, dismissing it entirely. As time went on, however, and as the voice grew with intensity, unfortunately, the boys began to listen.

"I've been thinking about it again," Gabriel said. "The Third keeps telling me to do it. I try to resist it, but it just gets louder and angrier."

Jackson nodded. "My voice has been talking to me all day. It didn't like that I was at the head doctor. It told me to grab a pencil and stab him and the bitch."

Gabriel smiled. "You should have done it. I bet it would feel good, seeing them die like that, them coughing blood into your face. His eyes went wide imagining the carnage. "That would make The Third happy."

The boys stood in silence, both imagining the kill, a craving that they had both yet to satisfy.

*"You can't trust him,"* Jackson's demonic darkness suddenly whispered. *"He thinks he is the strongest."*

*"Who?"* Jackson asked.

*"Him!"*

Jackson looked at his twin brother who was throwing more rocks.

*"But...he's my brother!"* Jackson thought.

*"He does not deserve to be with you. He is a lesser being, a mere imposter. He doesn't have the resolve! He lies to you!"* The voice hissed.

Jackson was unsure that he believed The Third's assessment of Gabriel." *I don't believe you,"* Jackson responded. *"He and I want the same things. We are a team."*

*"Foolish boy,"* The sinister voice said. *"It matters not if you believe me. You will see. He will overpower you if you aren't vigilant."*

"You ok?" Gabriel asked, startling Jackson from his internal conversation. "Yeah, I'm fine." Jackson said. Gabriel had scared all the remaining cats away and was now walking back towards the house. Jackson watched him.

*Is he lying to me?* He wondered. *Does he have my back like he says he does?*

*"Keep him close,"* The dark voice growled.

Jackson pursued his twin, and they chased each other till they reached the front door of the house. They entered and saw their mother preparing some sort of stew for supper. They walked past without acknowledging her and went through the common area into the back where the bedrooms were. They could hear the shower in their mother's room and could see Everett's clothes on her floor. Beside his worn boots, lay his black backpack. Looking towards the kitchen to see if they were being watched, Gabriel whispered to his brother. "Follow me."

The pair sneaked into their mother's bedroom and lifted the backpack onto the bed. They listened for signs that their mother was on the move, and in unison, they opened the bag and sifted through the contents. The bag contained nothing of real value or importance except a silver Zippo lighter and a folding knife with a three-inch blade.

"The knife is mine!" Gabriel said.

"I want it!" Jackson responded defiantly.

"You can have the lighter," Gabriel negotiated. "I'm taking the knife." And with that, he slid the knife into his pocket. The water in the shower had stopped and the boys could hear the curtain pull back. Jackson quickly put the lighter in his pocket and returned the bag to where they had found it. They slipped out of the room and went unnoticed into their own room as the bathroom door opened and Everett emerged with a towel around his waist. The boys then closed their door before their new guest could see them. The boys chuckled and went their separate ways in the bedroom before Gabriel heard a familiar hiss inside his head.

*"Why do you continue to socialize with that worm?"* The Third asked.

Gabriel looked at his brother who leaped onto his bed. *"Who? Jackson?"*

*"Yes, Jackson,"* The voice hissed. *"Haven't you realized that you are the strongest of the two of you? You are a lion in a family of sheep. Jackson is false, a fake. I have spoken to him, and I see no greatness, like I see in you. You should be in command of our fate, not Jackson, he lacks the apptitude."*

Gabriel pondered what the voice was telling him. *"You're saying that Jackson wants to be in charge over me?"*

*"Yes. But for now, watch him. The time will come when you can make your move."*

An hour later, Mrs. Trunt called the boys to the dinner table. Everett was already seated and had a large glass of water in front of him. The boys took up chairs either side of him and their mother began serving bowls of hot stew. As the table was finally set, Mrs. Trunt told them that she needed to use the restroom and excused herself. The boys looked at Everett and he was visibly uncomfortable. He attempted to say something to break the silence, but Gabriel beat him to it.

"You enjoying yourself yet?" he asked sarcastically.

"I'm sorry, what?" replied the young man.

"You must be enjoying yourself," said Gabriel. "With you wearing our dad's clothes and all. Sitting at his seat."

"Your mother said I could wear these while my own clothes got washed!" Everett said, incredulous of the crassness of the comment.

"You must really like it here," Jackson added. "Probably want to fuck her just like our dad too, huh."

"Gentlemen, I don't know what's going on," Everett defended. "All I know is that you have no right to talk to me like that. Your mother invited me in and I'm sorry if you don't like it but tough shit."

*"Kill him!"* The Third whispered to Jackson. *"Cut his throat!"*

"Oh! You hear that, Jackson!" Gabriel goaded. "He said "tough shit"! Well, I guess he's the man of the house now, we best not upset our new dad!"

Mrs. Trunt returned to the dining room. "Everybody getting along?" she asked, Everett smiled sheepishly, and the boys snickered to themselves.

"Just swell!" smirked Jackson.

The boys were silent for the entirety of the meal. Mrs. Trunt and Everett made small talk and he regaled her with his experiences in the Navy and the places he had traveled. They spoke at length about his family and how he came to be on his own. Mrs. Trunt seemed to be infatuated with the young man. She had to stop herself from staring at him. He had cleaned up nicely and was much more handsome than he was just a few hours earlier. Though she was twice his age, she couldn't help but feel a schoolgirl like attraction towards him. Her loneliness had peaked shortly after her husband died and she now felt herself yearning for this younger man that had unexpectedly entered her life. She felt as if she had disguised her interest in him well enough, but the boys were all too aware of what was going on and noticed it immediately. The conversation fell silent, and the meal was nearly complete when Mrs. Trunt said something unexpected by all at the table.

"Whattia think about staying around a while, Mr. Morrison?" She asked.

Jackson coughed on his Stew. Gabriel shot his mother a troubled look.

Everett, who seemed just as surprised, took a minute to answer. "Well, gee, Miss, that's gracious and all, but where would I stay?"

"Wait, wait, wait," Jackson said in disbelief. "Are you fucking kidding me? You just met this clown and now you want him to stay?"

"Jackson!" His mother snapped. "I have had about enough of your mouth today, go to your room!"

*"Kill him!"* The voice whispered.

"No, he's right, you fucking whore!" cried Gabriel, coming to the aid of his brother. "Dad hasn't even been dead for a year and now you're trying to replace him!"

*"KILL THEM BOTH!"* The Third demanded of Jackson.

"Listen you two," their mother said, rising to her feet. "I don't need your permission to do anything in MY house! And I am not trying to replace your father, I was going to ask Mr. Everett if he was interested in helping maintain the property in exchange for room and board, but you little assholes don't have the decency to let me finish!"

She sat back down and began to sniffle. "I wish you two weren't so awful to me. You never would have spoken to your father this way."

"Here come the water works!" sneered Jackson.

"Just leave us alone!" Mrs. Trunt screamed. "Go away!"

Filled with rage, Jackson stood and threw his empty bowl across the room and hit the wall. The bowl exploded into a hundred little pieces, and they scatted across the old hardwood floor.

Everett stood and backed away from the table. Jackson heard the voice again. *"Kill him! Cut his throat!"* He moved towards Everett but stopped. An idea had wormed its way into his brain. Gabriel looked on, anxiously.

*This isn't the time,* Jackson thought. He restrained himself and backed away from Everett who had pressed his back against the way, wary of an attack. Jackson flashed him a cold smile and left the table towards his room. Gabriel stood up and snarled at Everett.

"You touch her, you're fucking dead."

"Leave!" Their mother cried in between sobs.

Gabriel kicked over his chair and joined his brother in their shared bedroom.

"Can you believe that bitch!" Gabrielle said upon entering the room. Jackson was laying on the twin bed they both shared. Jackson sat up to look at his brother. "I almost did it Gabe. I almost killed him. The Third was telling me to do it, but I stopped."

"Why did you stop? I would have helped you." asked Gabriel.

Jackson motioned for his brother to close the bedroom door. They could hear their mother crying and Everett trying to console her. Gabriel did as his brother asked and closed the door. He then sat on the floor close to Jackson and looked up at him.

*"Tell him nothing! He'll betray us!"* The Third commanded.

*"We can trust him!"* Jackson said to his inner demon.

Jackson shared his plan with Gabriel. Gabriel grinned as the blueprint of Everett's removal unfolded. The two went back and forth into the night whispering different ideas until they agreed on a set course of action. They then turned out the lights and went to bed, counting the minutes till the next day.

Gabriel awoke early and rolled over to wake up his snoring brother. Jackson's eyes slammed open, and he shot upright. He looked over at Gabrielle and the twins nodded at each other.

*Let's do this.*

They rolled out of bed and quickly got dressed. Before leaving, the boys hugged. They knew what they were about to do would change everything. In their embrace they felt a surge of power flow between them. They had dreamed of this for months now. Their longing to quench the thirst was soon to be satisfied. The Third would finally be appeased. They separated and head butted each other, a gesture of encouragement.

The pair left their room and walked to the kitchen where their mother was bustling about, cooking breakfast.

Everett sat at the kitchen table and cringed as the boys entered. They sat in their seats on either side of Everett and smiled at him.

"Good morning," Jackson said, smiling politely.

Taken aback, Everett was silent. "How did you sleep?" asked Gabriel.

"Fine," Everett answered cautiously.

Mrs. Trunt walked into the room, wary of their presence. "You two leave him alone, understand?"

*"She doesn't control usss,"* The voice hissed.

*"NOT NOW,"* Jackson thought. *"You be quiet."*

*"Do not presume to command me, boy,"* The Third growled in his ear.

Jackson ignored the voice in his head and focused his attention on Everett. "I just want to say, my brother and

I talked it over, and we want to apologize for our behavior yesterday. It was not called for and we are sorry."

"Yeah," added Gabriel. "We have had a hard time since our dad died. We have issues with our anger and sometimes we just explode. I'm sorry too."

Everett smiled and let his guard down. "That's ok guys. It must be mighty strange having a new fella in the house. But trust me, I am not trying to be a dad just yet!" The group laughed and the tension from the day before melted away. They ate breakfast and afterwards, Mrs. Trunt prepared to leave for work.

"Why don't you boys show him around the property after you get your schoolwork finished?" Mrs. Trunt suggested. "Mr. Morrison has decided to stay with us a while so you guys can show him around and where the tools are and everything else."

"Please ma'am, call me Everett."

"Then you best call me Rebeca, not ma'am," She then gave him a coy smile and a wink. Jackson and Gabriel both saw their mother flirting with the newly hired hand. They did their best to hide their disgust and had to change the topic quickly.

"Yeah, we can show him the pond too!" Jackson said excitedly. "Do you like to fish, Everett?"

"Are you kidding? I love to fish. Ya'll got a pond here? What's in it?" Everett inquired.

"Mostly crappie and small mouth bass but some catfish too," Gabriel informed.

"You boys can take Everett to the pond AFTER you have done your schooling. Everett, don't let them trick you into going early." She looked at the trio. "I have to go to work now. Be good. Behave. Everett, my work number is on the counter if you need anything. I'll be back around four and I'll make supper." With that, Mrs. Trunt grabbed her purse and car keys and walked out the door. The group stood and watched as she turned her car around on the dirt driveway and sped off towards town.

"Fella's, I know she said wait until your schoolin' was done but I want to get to work as soon as possible. Make her happy, ya know? Hows about you show me around now? It'll be a chance for us to get to know each other better," Everett asked.

"Let's go to the pond first," suggested Gabriel. They all agreed, and the boys escorted Everett to a small tool shed out on the backside of the house. The boys grabbed their fishing poles and tackle boxes and proceed to the northern part of the property. As they walked, Everett told them about different species of fish he had seen while he was at sea and what some of them even tasted like. The boys pretended to be interested but their thoughts were occupied with more sinister intentions. After walking for a while, they were able to see the pond in the distance. It was not very big, but it did have some nice-looking trees surrounding it, making it appear more regal than it was.

They approached the water and Everett admired Trunt pond. There was a little dock that led from the shore to about ten feet into the water. The boys and Everett walked onto the dock and began preparing their fishing lines. Gabriel flashed Jackson a look as they were preparing their poles.

*It's time.*

"I gotta go take a piss. I'll be right back," Jackson said, walking off the dock and into the wood line.

Everett was knelt and looked through Jackson's tackle box. "You guys ain't got much in the way of lures, do you?" He asked.

"No. Not really," Gabriel said, not paying much attention to him.

Gabriel looked to the wood line and saw his brother creeping towards them with a large tree branch that had been cleared of the limbs and leaves. Jackson motioned for his brother to distract their target while he approached.

"Hey, Everett," Gabriel said, trying to not let his anticipation show. "Can you help me with this line? It's all tangled."

"Sure thing," Everett laughed.

Everett's back was now to the stealthy Jackson who inched closer, mindful of his footsteps so they would not give away his position. Gabriel was trembling with excitement. He could hardly hold still due to the adrenaline coursing through his veins.

Everett was oblivious to the danger he was in as he continued to untangle the line ensnared on Gabriel's reel. With each step Jackson crept closer, and with each passing moment he felt his heart pounding harder. His moment had finally come. Jackson was now three feet away from his target.

*"Kill, kill!"* The Third ordered. *"Spill his blood!"*

Jackson raised his club above his head and made eye contact with his brother who stood to the side of Everett. Gabriel gave his brother an encouraging nod and stepped away from Everett. Everett looked up from his task to see Gabriel stepping away and looking behind him. Everett turned to see what Gabriel was looking at, but it was too late.

*"KILL!"*

Jackson swung the club down with all of his strength. It connected with Everett's skull and glanced across his ear and down to his shoulder. The blood began pouring immediately as Everett crumpled to the ground, nearly unconscious. Jackson raised the branch again and swung at Everett who now began screaming in pain.

Gabriel removed the knife he stole from the backpack and opened it. With a vicious roar he stabbed Everett repeatedly in the torso and abdomen. The blood covered his hands and the knife glistened as it was thrust over and over into its victim's body. Everett was thrashing and crying out in pain, he tried to kick Gabriel, but his damaged coordination was no match for the merciless boys. Jackson continued to club violently at Everett's head until he was no longer making any noise. The boys cut and beat and stabbed the lifeless heap long after he had died. They finally stopped and stood over Everett's dead body. The boys were out of breath but still managed to laugh in unison. Their clothes were covered with blood spatter, and they delighted in watching the crimson liquid pour from the multitude of open wounds that adorned the body of Everett Morrison.

The Third had been appeased.

# TWELVE

The following Monday, Glenn woke up and got ready for work. His routine was always the same. Wake up. Start the coffee. Take a shower. Get dressed. Check the pistol. Drink the coffee. Feed the dog. Leave. The only difference in today's routine was that Mary wasn't around for him to speak to while he completed each task. Her presence was notably missed now, and Glenn desperately wanted to make things right with her. *I'll get some flowers after work.* Glenn drank his coffee while checking the weather on his phone.

*Another hot one*, he thought. His phone began to vibrate. There was an incoming call from a number he did not recognize. He cancelled the call and began reading the weather again. The phone rang again. It was the same number as before. Glenn cleared his throat and accepted the call.

"Detective Blackthorne," he said officially.

"Detective, this is Melanie Crix," said the voice on the other end. "Have you found anything on my sister?"

*Shit.* Glenn had almost forgotten his new case that came to him the previous Friday.

"No not yet," he said regretfully. "I apologize, I have had some personal issues come up this weekend and I wasn't able to follow up on the investigation. Have you received any other information?"

Melanie Crix was annoyed. "My sister has been missing for almost a week now, I do not care about your personal issues, Mr. Blackthorne!"

Glenn sighed. "I have not forgotten Isabelle, Miss Crix, but I also told you that I have other cases and responsibilities! However, since I haven't even left my home yet, I am going to see what information I can dig up before I go to the office, Ok?"

"I'm glad you can fit us into your busy schedule, Detective," Melanie snorted before promptly hanging up.

*Bitch.*

Glenn pocketed his phone and finished his coffee. *I gave her my word though.* He opened his notebook and reviewed the information he had taken when he first spoke to Melanie and was surprised to see that the gas station where Isabelle worked was only a couple blocks away from his own house.

*That makes it easy. At least, easier.*

He continued reading the notes:

Isabelle Anne Crix, twenty-four years old, five foot four, natural light blonde hair, blue eyes, fair complexion, approximately 125 pounds. Last seen by coworkers on Tuesday. Single tattoo of a bell wrapped in a red bow on left breast, no known alias, no history of drug abuse, no current significant other. One known arrest for assault in 2020. Works at Kum and Go gas station on South Orchard Street. Physical address is same as sister, Melanie Crix.

Satisfied with the review, Glenn closed his notebook and returned it to his pocket. He took is cellphone and dialed the main office number for The Detective Division. The phone rang twice.

"Investigations, this is Denise, how may I help you today?"

"Denise, its Glenn."

"Oh, hi Glenn!" Her voice became more personable. "How is everything? A little bird told us that something had happened and that's why you had to leave early."

*Kimmy,* Glenn thought.

"Yeah, I got a call that my dad had passed away."

"That's what the little birdy told me," Denise said.

"Would this little birdy be named Kimmy Lee by any chance?" Questioned Glenn.

"I don't reveal my sources," Denise said playfully.

Glenn couldn't help but smile. Denise was one of the finest people he had ever known. Playful and genuine, Denise Young was a good friend that Glenn knew he could trust and rely on. He had just been promoted to Detective when she was first hired by the department. The two hit it off immediately and it has been a close friendship ever since.

Well, Mrs. Young, I'm just calling to let you know that I will most likely be out of the office for most of the day. I have plenty of follow up work scheduled. My phone is charged and on if anyone needs to get ahold of me." Glenn advised.

"Ok, where are you going to be located?" asked Denise.

"All over Denise, you know how this goes. The whole city is my playground."

"Where…Are…You…Going…To…be…located…Detective…Blackthorne?" Denise articulated authoritatively. She was very concerned about her coworkers and insisted on knowing where they were going in the event they needed help or got into trouble. Not that there was much she could do, but she took to the roll of acting as the office mom.

Glenn knew there was no sense in arguing and relinquished the information. "Kum and Go on South Orchard Street. I will let you know when I'm finished, ok mom?"

"Don't you sass me young man!" Densie said jokingly. "Just because you are bigger than me doesn't mean I can't whoop ya!"

Glenn chuckled. Maybe if things had worked out differently, he could see himself and Denise being together. But he was already married when they first met, and he loved his wife very much. Still, it was fun to think about alternate timelines.

"Have a good day, Denise," Glenn said.

"You too, Glenn. Take care. If you need anything, let me know."

"Will do." He hung up the phone and focused his attention back to the issue at hand: Finding out what happened to Isabelle Crix.

Glenn left his home and climbed into his vehicle. The Kum and Go gas station was a mere five-minute drive from where he lived. He arrived at the gas station and parked his vehicle in a stall close to the front doors. He exited his car, ensuring that his cellphone and notebook were still in his pocket, before he entered the store. As he passed through the front doors, a wafting smell of fresh coffee and assorted "grab and go" breakfast foods filled his nose and made his stomach rumble. He hadn't eaten yet today and was regretting it.

He walked to the cashier's counter and saw a young hispanic woman, about eighteen to nineteen years old, staring at her phone. The girl saw Glenn's approach and put her phone in her pocket and as enthusiastically as a teenager who works at a gas station could be, asked, "What can I do for you today, sir?"

"Howdy," Glenn said. "I'm Detective Blackthorne with the Tulsa Police Department. I'm here to investigate Isabelle Crix's disappearance." The young woman eyed Glenn carefully.

"I haven't seen her since last Tuesday. She really screwed me over, not showing up for work, I had a vacation planned with my boyfriend and when she didn't show up, I had to cover all her shifts," the woman said, unamused.

"I'm sorry to hear that," Glenn said flatly. "Sounds like it sucks. What's your name, Miss?"

"Am I a suspect or something? Because I hardly knew her," The woman asked defensively.

"No, not at all, I am just conducting a follow up investigation, and I like to have the information of the people I talk to for my report. You're not in trouble at all."

Glenn knew the importance of keeping people relaxed during a field interview. The calmer they felt, even if they were a suspect, they usually would divulge more information. Not letting someone know that they are being investigated or under suspicion is a technique utilized by police in order to keep a person talking and maybe slip up and admit to something.

The girl was quiet for a second. "Kristen. Kristen Ramirez." she finally said.

Glenn removed his notebook and wrote her name down. "Ok, Kristen, what's your birthday?"

"February 18, 2004."

"Good address? Phone number?" Glenn asked.

"Why do you need this stuff? I thought you said I wasn't in trouble," Kristen exclaimed, her eyes narrowing. "Are you some kind of perv or something?" she asked, raising her voice. "You're probably not even a real cop!"

Without hesitation, Glenn pulled back his suit jacket and showed the argumentative young woman his Detective's badge worn close to his department issued pistol. Glenn raised his eyebrows at her and asked, "Does this answer your question?"

"It's probably fake!" Kristen said. "I get a lot of pervy guys hitting on me all the time and they get creative in how they get my info!"

Glenn started to lose his patience. "Look, that's a real badge and I'm a real police detective. I need you to give me the information I'm asking for, or you are going to be at risk of interfering with my investigation, and then you WILL be in trouble. Understood?"

Glenn could see the defiance in Kristen starting to break down. She rolled her eyes but relented and gave him her address and phone number. A line was beginning to form behind Glenn and the manager came out to see what was happening.

"Kristen!" The man said. "What's going on? There are customers waiting!" He looked at Glenn who was writing in his notepad.

"Is this guy giving you trouble?"

"You can say that," Glenn said with a smirk. "I'm Detective Blackthorne, Tulsa Police. Are you the manager?"

"Yes," The man said timidly. "My name is John. I'm the General Manager."

"Good to meet you, John," Glenn said, extending his hand. John returned the greeting, and they shook hands. "I'm looking to get some information on one of your employees. If you have a minute, I would like to discuss somethings with you…" Glenn looked back at the curious faces of the customers in the store. "In private."

"Of course! Kristen, you make sure these people are taken care of and when you're finished, clean the restrooms. The men's room looks like a refugee camp," John said. Kristen gave him a look of disgust but turned to help the next customer in line.

"Let's talk in my office," John said, guiding Glenn to the back room. The two walked to the door the manager had first appeared from and Glenn went in first. It was a cramped room full of paperwork and a small desk. A tv monitor displayed six different camera views from inside the store and the parking lot. Cardboard boxes of old products and invoices littered the floor and employee schedules, and a calendar of upcoming events were on an old bulletin board behind the overflowing desk.

"Excuse the mess," The manager said, kicking a box out of the way. "Have a seat."

He motioned for Glenn to sit in the rickety chair in front of the desk. Glenn sat and had to catch himself after the chair felt as if it were buckling beneath his weight. Glenn readjusted himself so the chair wasn't as wobbly and watched as John fought with his own chair.

"The company not too fond of buying new chairs?" Glenn asked.

John smiled sheepishly. "I'm still what you would call a rookie here, officer. I have only been the manager for about three weeks. I'm still learning how to run this place, much less, how to ask for new equipment."

Glenn nodded and opened his notebook back up. "I'm here because there was a concern about Isabelle Crix from a family member. She said that she hasn't been home in a week, which is unusual, and that her coworkers said that the last time they saw her was last Tuesday. What can you tell me about Isabelle, and do you have any other information I can use to determine what happened?"

John sat up in his chair. "I remember some crazy woman coming in asking about Isabelle last week and she was screaming and hollering, and I finally had to tell her to leave. She said she was her sister."

"She's the one who called me," Glenn answered. "Who was working the last day Isabelle was here?"

John pondered the question for a moment. "Let's see, on Tuesday it was me, Kristen, Isabelle, and Tammy."

"Is Tammy here today?" Glenn asked.

"No," replied John. "She usually works evenings and nights. If there was anyone to talk to about Isabelle, it's Tammy Shard. Her and Belle- she liked to be called Belle- were always laughing and having fun. They seemed to be really close."

Glenn began jotting down the information. "You said her name is Tammy Shard? I'm assuming that's short for Tamara?

John nodded. Glenn continued to write in his notebook. "John, I'm going to need your contact information and the contact information of your employees. Especially Tamara Shard. You said they were close? Did she ever mention where she might think Isabelle is?"

John shrugged. "All I know is that on Tuesday evening, Tammy and Belle were on shift together and they talked about having a drink after work and left together. When Isabelle didn't show up for her shift the next day, I asked Tammy if she knew anything and all she told me was that Belle came over, had a few drinks, and went home. I assumed it was a no call-no show."

*This is odd,* Glenn thought. *The friend says that she went home after drinking but the sister said she never showed. She didn't come to work the next day, either.*

"John, do you know if Isabelle has any drug history or has a boyfriend she might be staying with? Any reason at all that she wouldn't go home?"

John shrugged again. "I really don't know, Detective. Like I said before, I'm brand new here and haven't gotten to know everyone well enough yet. But Tamara is the one I'd talk to if I needed to know something about Isabelle."

"I plan to do just that," Glenn said. "Please give me her contact information."

The manager gave Glenn his own personal information and Tamara's. Glenn gave John a couple of his business cards and advised him to give them to his other employees and if they had any other information, to give him a call. John stood and accepted the cards and sat back in his chair. As he sat, the old chair decided that today was the day, and one of the rear legs broke, causing John to tumble backwards onto the floor. Glenn had to turn away to contain his laughter.

After Glenn finished speaking with the manager, he stepped into the main area of the gas station, where he saw Kristen Ramirez angrily walking a mop bucket into the men's restroom. Glenn continued out the door and into his car, where his removed his cell phone and dialed a number.

"Yellow," said Detective Meyer.

"Lemon, I need you to run some names for me."

# THIRTEEN

"Stop! leave me alone!" Santina screamed; her long hair was in a tangled bundle in the clenched fist of Sally Mosenteen. The gathering group of children laughed as they witnessed the torment of their peer at the hands of the cruel Sally.

"You like getting me in trouble, don't you stupid!" Sally sneered at the whimpering Santina, who had now fallen to her knees to try and alleviate the pain in her head.

"Nnn nnooo!" Santina yelped. "It was an accident!" Just moments before, in the school cafeteria, Santina had inadvertently bumped into Sally as she was carrying her tray of food, and it had spilled into a large mess on the floor. Sally was quickly reprimanded by a teacher.

"The teacher said I did it on purpose!" cried Sally, pulling hard with both hands now. "They are going to give me detention! My dad is going to kill me and it's all your fault!" After being scolded by the lunchroom supervisor, Sally had followed Santina to the playground as she began to mount her swing. Before unsuspecting Santina could sit, she felt her hair go taught, and was yanked out of the seat by a furious Sally Mosenteen.

"Please stop!" Santina pleaded. *Pwease Stawp.*

"I'll at least have a reason for detention!" Sally screamed as she began pummeling the top of Santina's head. The crowd roared and it fueled Sally's rage. At that moment, all went quiet in Santina's mind. She was outside of her body, looking down at the beating she was receiving. An overwhelming hatred took hold of her of her thoughts, she thought of Jackson and how he had hurt her and how her momma had treated her. She thought of the cruelty of

Sally and Connor and something deep inside finally snapped.

*No more. Not ever.*

With all her strength, Santina lunged forward and secured Sally's left leg with both her arms and drove forward. Caught off guard, Sally immediately let go of Santina's hair and braced for the inevitable fall. The crowd went silent as Santina released her grip and climbed on top of Sally and began raining down fists into her face. Santina cursed and screamed, imagining every horrible thing that had happened to her, every insecurity and how she was ridiculed mercilessly. Sally flailed and tried to get away, but Santina was on the warpath and wanted revenge.

As quickly as it all started, the school faculty rushed to the brawl and separated the girls. Sally was crying and her face was bloodied from the barrage of strikes inflicted by Santina. Santina began to weep uncontrollably as she was escorted to the principal's office of the school.

Tamara Shard was admiring her black eye in her bathroom mirror. The pain had gone away but there was still noticeable discoloration.

*That piece of shit,* she thought to herself as she began applying makeup to the bruised eye. She didn't have to go to work for a couple hours, but the unsightly appearance of her face was a disturbing reminder of who she lived with. *That motherfucker.*

Tamara and Jackson had met a year ago in a bar called the Rock Hard, and Tamara was immediately smitten. Jackson was handsome and tall, and she loved his tattoos that covered his body. Jackson had told her that he was recently laid off from working in the Texas oilfields as a roughneck and moved to Oklahoma for a new job site, but that he did have some money saved up. Never one to pass up a chance at money, after a couple of weeks, Tamara invited Jackson to live with her and Santina.

At first, things were great. Jackson shared gave her money, and she gave him a place to stay. Over time though, Jackson continued to not work, and his money eventually dried up. He claimed that he was waiting for an oil contract in western Oklahoma, but Tamara didn't believe him. Jackson had mysteriously taken over the basement cellar for reasons unknown to her and forbid her and Santina from ever going down there. Whenever she heard a strange noise emanating from the cellar door, Jackson dismissed it and said it must have been rats or a raccoon. Although charming in the beginning Jackson started to become more aggressive as the days passed. Their once passionate escapades in the bedroom now had evolved into a sadistic nightmare, where Jackson would reach euphoria by causing pain, no matter how degrading or uncomfortable it was to Tamara.

She began to regret letting him stay and once had told him that he needed to leave. Jackson whipped her with a belt and ordered her to always obey him. After that, Tamara began to fear him and what he was capable of. He later on would start regularly beating her if she crossed him.

Recently, to Tamara's horror, Jackson professed to her that he wondered what it would be like if they murdered someone together. The comment terrified Tamara, and she tried to pack a bag and leave the home, but Jackson attacked her and tied her up so she couldn't go and threatened to kill her if she ever tried to leave again. The psychological and physical abuse became too much, and her resistance turned into cooperation for her own survival. She agreed that she would help Jackson find someone to kill but didn't know where to begin…until she met Isabelle at work. Isabelle was new to the store and needed a friend. When Tamara described her to Jackson, he told her to do whatever it took to gain her trust and to bring her to the house.

Tamara finished applying her make up when she received a text on her cell phone from her manager, John. She disliked the wimpy little man, but unfortunately, she had the pleasure of working for him. Looked out of her bedroom and saw Jackson sleeping on the bed and tiptoed past him and into the living room. She sat on the couch and lit a cigarette before dialing John's number.

"This is John."

"You wanted me to call?" Tamara asked.

"Hi, Tammy, listen, I just had a police detective here a little while ago, and he was asking around about Belle."

Tamara felt ice fill her veins. She went silent and was horrified at the thought of the police wanting to speak to her about Isabelle.

"You still there?" John asked.

Still stunned, Tamara answered. "Yeah. What do they want to talk to me about? I don't know where she is."

Tamara knew all too well where Isabelle was.

"Look, he asked for your phone number, and I gave it to him. Just try and cooperate and tell him what you know."

"But I don't know anything!" She protested.

At that moment, Tamara felt the uneasy feeling of being watched by something she couldn't see. The hair on her neck raised and a primal discomfort crept down her spine. She turned slowly and saw Jackson looming over her. His terrifying presence scared her speechless.

*How was he so quiet!*

Tamara hung up the phone and looked up at Jackson, who was punishing her with his eyes.

"Who was that?" he asked in a dangerous voice.

Tamara quickly thought of a lie.

"It was… my brother. He wanted to know what nursing home our mother was in."

Jackson stood still, hardly blinking. His chest hardly seemed to move as he breathed.

*"She lies to you!"* The Third screeched.

Jackson studied Tamara's face that was now pale from fear. "I'm going to ask you again," he growled ominously.

"Who was that?"

"Santina, I am very disappointed with your behavior. It is not like you at all to be picking fights." Principle Adams scolded. Santina sat in one of the two chairs in front of the principles desk. Sally Mosenteen sat in the other chair, holding a paper towel to her bloodied face. "Sally is bleeding, and you may very well have broken her nose!"

Santina was still sniffling. No one had asked for her side of the story.

"She," Santina stuttered. "Sheeee hhhuurrt me first."

"Every student we spoke to said that YOU started the altercation. They said that you had first threw Sally's tray down in the lunchroom, then went outside and fought with her."

"That's not true!" Santina shrieked, her stutter vanishing.

"Do NOT raise your voice at me young lady," The principal warned.

Frustrated, Santina decided not to argue. She did get in a fight after all. Who cares who started it.

"Santina, I have tried calling your mother, but the number we have on file is no longer active. Do you know if she has a new phone number?"

Santina shook her head. "She has a new phone, but I don't know that number."

The principle was annoyed. "Well seeing as you are under suspension, I can't keep you at the school, but I want to speak to your parents. You normally walk home, correct?"

"Yes," Santina responded.

"Ok. When you get home, have your mother call me. Ok?"

"Yes sir," Santina mumbled.

"Santina you are suspended for three days, that means you cannot be on school property at all during that period," Principal Adams said. "That includes swinging on the swing set after school hours."

Santina felt a pang of sadness radiate through her. That was her safe place.

"Yes sir," she repeated.

"You may go."

Santina stood and before leaving, shot a glance at Sally. Sally looked away quickly. Santina left and grinned on her way out the front doors.

Tamara couldn't breathe with Jackson's strong hand wrapped against her throat.

"It was my brother..." she gasped, "I swear!"

*"Squeeeezzeee,"* The Third ordered. *"Squeeze till she tells us the truth."*

Tamara's phone rang. It was lying on the couch where Tamara had set it before she was snatched by Jackson. He reached over and secured it without letting go of Tamara's throat. She winced and struggled against his powerful grip. Jackson looked at the caller ID.

Unknown Number

*"Let's see who she's been talking to,"* hissed the voice.

Jackson raised a finger to his lips to signal for Tamara to remain silent.

Jackson pressed the accept call key and listened.

"Hello?" A man's voice said.

Jackson was silent, ensuring his breathing did not reveal him.

"Hello?" Said the voice again. "Tamara? This is Detective Blackthorne with the Tulsa Police Department."

"Tell him you can't talk right now," Jackson whispered and handed the phone to her, only slightly loosening his grip. Tamara grabbed the phone with a trembling hand and answered.

"I'm sorry Detective but I can't talk right now."

"This will only take a minute, Tamara," said the man.

"I can't talk now," her voice breaking. Jackson snatched the phone from her hand and ended the call. Tamara felt Jacksons grip tighten again, harder this time. She pulled and wriggled but couldn't get free.

"So now the police are involved. That's disappointing Tamara, I thought you could keep a secret," Jackson said.

"I…haven't…told…anyone!" Tamara gasped.

*"Kill…her…"* The Third ordered.

"You know that I will have to kill you now, right? Your daughter too. You both have seen too much." Jackson furrowed his brow, Tamara continued to struggle. He grabbed her throat with both hands and threw her to the ground and mounted her. Tamara kicked and fought but he was too heavy and was incredibly strong. The light was beginning to fade, and Tamara began to see stars. Jackson leaned his weight into his hands, causing Tamara to flail wildly, knocking over the coffee table in front of the couch, spilling cigarette buts and beer cans to the floor.

"Do you think Isabelle was my first?!" Jackson roared as he continued to strangle Tamara's throat. "There have been many others! You have just been a cover for me!" Tamara was no longer able to fight back, the lack of oxygen had made her docile and weak. She clung to life for as long as she could.

"I do as The Third tells me!" He howled before willing more strength from his massive hands to further crush her windpipe.

Tamara went limp. Jackson eased off her throat and breathed deeply as he admired his work. The fire in his lungs was his reward for a job well done and Tamara's lifeless body lay wide eyed on the floor beneath him. He felt a delicious surge of power jolt through him.

*I am a God.*

Jackson stood and continued to watch her, ensuring that she was no longer breathing. He heard the rustle of chains at the basement door. He looked at the door and back down at Tamara. "I think it's about time you came down to the cellar."

## FOURTEEN

*It's not fair,* Santina thought as she walked home from school. *I didn't start it! It was Sally's fault!* Santina continued her walk to the bent stop sign, turned, and ambled down the block towards her home. She grumbled as she walked, thinking of the injustice that had been done. *What's momma gonna say?* Santina was frightened that momma was going to punish her harshly when she returned home early because of a fight. Santina rehearsed what she was going to say but it never came out as good as she wanted it to. *I wish I was on my swing. That would help me think.*

She turned up the sidewalk towards her home and navigated the creaky wooden staircase and attempted to open the door. *Locked.* Santina had a spare key in her backpack and used it to unlock the door. She twisted the handle and entered the dimly lit living room. She was expecting to see her mother sitting on the couch watching the television, but she wasn't there. *She must be asleep,* she thought, closing the door softly. Santina reached to the right of the door and fumbled her fingers, attempting to find the main light switch for the living room. She eventually found it and when the light shone brightly, she was dumbfounded by what she saw.

The floor was covered in cigarette ash and old beer cans. The coffee table that had once held the myriad of items had been turned on its side and a good two feet from where it normally sat. Momma's cell phone was laying just next to the couch and the screen appeared to be cracked. Santina wondered if momma knew that this mess was here and if Jackson had made it.

"Mmmmomma?" Santina asked softly, trying not to wake her mother if she didn't have to. She padded slowly across the carpet and into the hallway, where she saw the light on in her mother's bedroom.

*She must be asleep.*

Intent on keeping her mother calm for as long as possible, Santina decided that she would go to her own room until her mother awoke on her own. She started down the hall but stopped when she noticed something strange. She took a few steps back and observed that the cellar door was unlocked and slightly ajar. There was a foul odor coming from the cracked door, and she thought she could hear muffled voices.

*Best to leave it alone. Jackson will be angry if he finds out.*

She wanted to walk away but curiosity was getting the better of her. She wondered what Jackson did down there ever since he moved in and claimed it as his own.

*Just a little peek.*

She walked to the end of the hall to make sure that momma wasn't waking up. The room was in disarray as normal, but momma wasn't in it. *Did she go to work already?* As quietly as she could, Santina inched her way back to the cellar door. She slowly opened the door and slipped inside.

The stairs were nearly invisible, and the smell was awful. It was the most terrible stink she had ever smelt in her whole life. Nearing complete darkness, there was only the soft ambient light of a candle sitting on a table on the wall furthest from the stairs. She could hear a voice now, speaking softly in the darkness. She carefully walked further down the stairs, trying to stay as silent as possible, and peered over the railing to see the rest of the room. Her stomach dropped and she was instantly mortified at what appeared in front of her.

Jackson was sitting in a chair in the middle of the room with his back to the staircase. A human body laid at his feet and there was a…*creature*… kneeling over top of the body. Jackson was whispering soothing words to the hideous beast while petting its head like a dog. The monster was shackled to a great chain fastened to a collar around its neck. The beast was drooling and licking at the face of the body at Jackson's feet. Santina felt as if she was going to be sick at the sight of the ritual that was unfolding in front of her. Jackson continued to whisper to the beast while it grunted and clawed at the woman on the floor.

*Wait…* Santina thought, *that looks like…*

"Momma!" She gasped involuntarily, trying to cover her mouth.

Jackson stood quickly and turned to look at her on the staircase. His face was filled with surprise and his eyes burned with hatred. The creature, still kneeling, turned its head from Tamara Shard's body and looked at Santina with an angry growl, its grey lips curled back, baring rotten teeth in a vicious snarl.

Terrified of what she had seen, Santina scrambled up the stairs to safety, while Jackson charged up after her. Santina reached the doorway and slammed the door shut, and as quickly as she could, secured the padlock to the latch of the doors locking assembly. As she slammed the lock shut, Jackson crashed into the door causing it to shake violently.

"Santina!" Jackson roared as he smashed into the door again. "Santina! Get back here you little bitch!" The petrified Santina stepped away from the door and tried to catch her breath.

"Www…wwhat was that?" She asked herself. Jackson continued pounding on the door and Santina could see that the door's hinges were starting to loosen from Jackson's immense force. *I have to do something!* She thought as she ran into the living room. Her brain was in survival mode and was incapable of complex thought.

*Run…no, fight!...no… I don't know what to do!*

Santina searched her surroundings for a weapon while Jackson beat on the door, cursing and screaming at her. She couldn't find a suitable tool for defense, and she began to panic until she saw her mother's cell phone sitting on the floor by the couch. She scrambled to get to it but at that moment the cellar door gave way and Jackson's powerful body emerged, his head sweeping left and right, searching for her. Santina screamed and bolted for the front door, Jackson just behind her. She reached the door and grabbed the doorknob, but the backpack she was still wearing was yanked hard and she flew to the floor. She scrambled to get to her feet, but Jackson kicked her hard in the ribs. She crawled tried to crawl away from him, but Jackson jumped on top of her and began hitting her on the head. Santina screamed and squirmed to get away, but her assailant was too strong. He rolled her to her back, and wrapped his enormous hands around her tiny throat and began to squeeze. His face was pursed into a demonic gaze as he continued to strangle her.

Santina struggled against the man's weight, but she could hardly move him.

*I am going to die!*

Santina looked into her killer's face and saw him for the evil filth that he was and knew that she was finished. Just as she was about to give up, the same voice entered her head as it did earlier during her fight at school. She was outside of her body observing the hulking figure strangling her body.

*No more. Not ever. Fight!*

With the last bit of strength she could summon, Santina arched her hips as high as she could off the floor. The movement caused Jackson's weight to shift forward and before he could equalize it again, Santina brought her knee up hard, and smashed it into Jackson's groin. Jackson cried out in pain and immediately let go of Santina's throat before rolling off her, writhing in agony. Fresh air entered her lungs, and she coughed deeply as she scurried to her feet. Jackson, sensing his prey was escaping, stood as quickly as he could but not before Santina had flown out the front door. She was running as fast as she could back towards the school. *Someone there will help me!*

Jackson stumbled out the front door into the daylight and onto the porch steps. The force of his movement snapped the old planks and the whole staircase gave way and he tumbled to the ground. He watched as Santina disappeared out of sight. He rose again and charged towards where he had last seen her.

Santina's lungs were burning but the adrenaline made her run faster and further than she ever thought she could. She passed the bent stop sign and sprinted to the school. Jackson was two blocks behind and gaining fast. Santina ran to a side door of the school and banged as hard as she could, hoping someone would answer it in time. Jackson was closing the distance, so Santina abandoned the school and ran down the street away from her pursuer. *Where do I go!* She wondered, feeling the fatigue in her legs set in. *I don't know where to…*

*The Cop! Yes, the cop who was so nice to me the other day! Where did he live?*

She couldn't remember the address as she ran. The best she could do was run in the direction the man had pointed to when he told her where he lived. She headed down the block into the residential neighborhood where the nice man said his house was. Jackson was tiring as well and his pursuit had slowed but he was still moving towards her, cautious to not draw too much attention. Santina ran along a row of houses till she came to an intersection and looked at the street sign that said: Osage Street.

*That's not it,* she thought and turned right, running past more houses. She looked behind and couldn't see Jackson anymore, but she didn't dare stop. She ran to another intersection and saw a welcoming sight.

*Carson Way! It's 228 Carson Way, I remember now!*

Willing a final burst of speed from her tired legs, Santina sprinted down Carson Way, carefully searching for the 228 address. She had thought she had gone the wrong way when at the end of the block, she saw a large white house with a big driveway and mailbox lettered 228. Santina ran up the driveway to the front door and pounded with all her might.

"Let me in! Help!"

There was no answer, but there was an incredibly deep woofing sound that echoed from within. She banged again but stopped when she saw a figure running down the street towards her location. Panicking, Santina looked for a place to hide before Jackson could spot her. She crouched and shuffled back to the driveway where she saw two large garbage cans sitting next to the garage. Jackson was getting closer, and she knew it wouldn't be long before he found her again. Moving with haste, Santina opened the lid to the garbage can and crawled in, just as Jackson was reaching the house. She held her hands over her mouth to muffle her breathing and she could hear Jackson's footsteps slow to a walk. Her heart was pounding, and her lungs begged for air, but she didn't dare move her hands. She heard Jackson start moving again up the street and then turn around and return the way he came. She heard him curse loudly and then he disappeared.

    Santina waited for what felt like an eternity before she was brave enough to open the lid and peer out. It was getting late, and the sky was turning purple, but there was no sign of Jackson. Knowing that he could be anywhere, she slowly closed the lid and relaxed in the heap of garbage beneath her. She was exhausted and the adrenaline had worn off and she felt herself thinking back to the image of her momma lying on the floor underneath the creature. She sobbed silently, afraid to make too much noise, and thanked God that she was still alive.

# FIFTEEN

### Amarillo-2008

*"My brother, my own brother!"*

*"I warned you, boy, he would betray us."*

*"Yes, yes, you are ALWAYS right about everything, aren't you?! Look at the mess we are in. You could have spoken up sooner!"*

*"I spoke to you when you were just a child, I TOLD you to watch him; to keep him at bay, but no, you didn't heed my warnings."*

Jackson padded around the small room, brushing the walls with his shoulder until he reached a corner, and then pivoting to continue following the walls. There was a small bed adjacent to the far wall and a door that could only be unlocked from the outside. The room was used for suicide watch and belonged to a mental ward of an unknown hospital, Jackson didn't remember the trip, he only remembered waking up in the small room. He had a dream that one of the doctors was speaking to him…was it a dream? He did not know. He just knew that he had been betrayed by the one who was supposed to be there for him. The one person who was closest to him all his life. His brother, Gabriel.

"Why don't you mind your own damn business, Gabe," the conversation had begun earlier that day. "And don't act like you fucking care so much about me, you have been plotting against me ever since The Third came into our lives!"

"Jackson, I just bailed your stupid ass out of jail. Again. If you would get a damn job instead of fucking off and spending all of our money on stupid shit, maybe we could get the hell out of here!"

Gabriel moved closer to his drunk brother, who was visibly swaying in their apartment living room. Jackson had a mean look in his eye and reeked of cheap whiskey.

"I obviously care about you, you dumbass, otherwise, I wouldn't have looked out for you all these years! If I didn't care, why would I bail you out of jail?"

"I've bailed you out, too," Jackson muttered.

"Yeah, I know you have," Gabriel said softly. "The thing is, we are all we have in this world. We need to work together, like we use to do."

Jackson took another drink from the bottle he was holding and sighed heavily. He swayed and sat down hard on the old leather couch that took up most of the tiny living room.

"I don't like feeling this way anymore, Gabe. I hate having this voice in my head all the time. You still have it, don't you?"

Gabriel sat next to his brother on the couch, the sudden impact sent a small cloud of dust into the air. "Yeah, sometimes I still hear it. But to be honest with you, I just ignore it anymore. It has gotten easier since I quit drinking and doin all the drugs. I feel like I'm in control now. At least, somewhat."

"*He was too weak to wield me,*" The Third said.

"*I wish I could be rid of you too,*" lamented Jackson.

"*Then do it you coward!*" The Third roared in his ear. "*Do it and stop your complaining! You could have been great, but now…you are lesser than I could have ever imagined! Just do it! End it now!*"

"No, no, no!" Jackson screamed aloud as he threw his whiskey bottle across the room and clutched the side of his head with his hands. "I can't do it anymore, Gabriel! I can't do it anymore. It's egging me on. It says the only way to get rid of it is to kill myself! Is that what I have to do?"

Gabriel looked into his brother's pain-soaked eyes, understanding full well what he was going through. He had once been under The Third's dark spell and had narrowly escaped, but not before committing an atrocious act…the drifter… the blood… it sickened him to remember it. He could only speak of the foul secret to Jackson, but his brother was becoming more and more unstable as he succumbed to the influence of The Third. Gabriel knew not why he had a sudden change of heart or why he was being spared from the demon voice, unlike his poor brother, but all he knew was that he needed to protect his brother, at all costs.

Gabriel addressed his brother. "You try and relax. Get some sleep. I'll wake you up in a little while and we can go eat, ok? We can discuss our future later. But right now, you need to sober up."

Jackson wanted to protest, but after a long night in jail and half a bottle of rot-gut whiskey, he was ready for some proper sleep. He laid his head on the pillow Gabriel provided and closed his eyes. Gabriel stood and walked away from the couch, but as he did, he heard Jackson mumble softly, "Dad would have been proud of you." Gabriel's eyes went misty as he watched his brother stir slightly and begin snoring softly on the couch. He crept quietly into the kitchen where he removed a blue and gold rosary from his pocket and gripped it tightly.

"Heavenly Father," he whispered as he closed his eyes, "give me the strength to carry on. Give me the patience to be a better man. Absolve me of my sins, for there are many. Help my brother fight the demon that plagues his mind. And, most of all Father… help Jackson forgive me for what I am about to do."

Jackson awoke to the sound of heavy knocking on their front door. He tried sitting up, but he was still too drunk to control his movements, and instead, rolled his body so that he could see the door. He tried wiping the sleep from his eyes, when he saw his brother walk to the front door and open it, not even asking who it was first. Standing in the doorway, were two Amarillo police officers, and Gabriel was speaking softly to them. Jackson mustered the strength to sit up, becoming lightheaded as he did, as Gabriel invited the officers into the apartment, who moved quickly over to where Jackson sat.

"What the hell is all this about?" Jackson asked. "I just got out this morning, I haven't even had time to get in trouble again."

One of the officers, a Hispanic man of average build, spoke up first. "We got a report that you were suicidal and that we needed to come check on you. Have you thought of hurting yourself or anyone else today?"

Jackson looked quizzically at Gabriel who was standing side by side with the officers now. "Gabe, what the hell is going on?"

"You told me earlier that the.... voice, was telling you to kill yourself," Gabriel said. "I think it's best that you go to the hospital and get some help."

"Fuck that!" Jackson cried as he tried to stand. "I'd rather blow my head off than go to that place!"

"So, you are having harmful thoughts?" The second officer asked rudely.

"Yeah, towards you!" Jackson yelled. The officers swiftly grabbed Jackson by his enormous wrists and tried pinning him to the couch. Jackson flailed and cursed as they attempted to handcuff him. He was nearly successful at thwarting their efforts, before he felt another set of hands assisting the officers pin his hands behind his back. Looking behind him, he saw Gabriel grabbing his arms and yanking them to the small of his back, to the gratitude of the officers.

"You fucking traitor!" Jackson snarled; pure hatred filled his eyes. "You are no brother of mine!"

"Jackson, calm down!" pleaded Gabriel, "it will be ok, I promise! It's for your own good, you'll see!"

"Fuck you!" cried Jackson as he tried charging at his brother, the officers quickly pulling him back. "I will get you back for this!"

That was the last moment that Jackson remembered. He was so deeply filled with rage and liquor, that the ride to the hospital was a blur that he could not recollect. Now he sat in his tiny room, castaway in thought, mourning the betrayal of his brother.

"*You act surprised,*" the little voice hissed, "*you were always stronger than him. We all knew it, even your* brother. That's why he has sent you here, to this...cage. He wants me for himself, don't you see? Those lies that he said about not hearing me anymore? Nonsense."

Jackson stared aimlessly at the floor; the light flickered overhead. *"He said that he cares for me, then he goes and does this."*

*"This is temporary,"* The Third said. *"You must find a way for him to never be able to do this to us again. A final solution, if you will."*

*"You mean I should kill him?"* Jackson asked.

*"Yes,"* The Third hissed. *"Afterall, he has betrayed you, betrayed... US! That cannot be permitted to stand."*

Jackson felt the anger welling up inside him again. *"Why did he have to do this? He destroyed the trust between brothers. I thought I could count on him! I shared everything with him and then he does this to me. Puts me in the crazy house and says it's for my own good! If I had it my way, he would be locked away too!"*

The Third was silent for a moment before whispering, *"That can be arranged."*

For the rest of the evening, the voice and the man discussed at length what they were going to do to enact their revenge. The hours clicked by as the silent conversation took place in the tiny room.

Seventy-two hours later, after the mandatory psychiatric hold was over, Jackson was released from the hospital and was surprised to see Gabriel in the parking lot, leaning back on his green Ford Taurus. Jackson felt the hair on the back of his neck rise at the sight of his traitorous brother.

*"Easy, remember what we discussed,"* The Third said. Jackson forced his anger back down and was even

able to manage a weak smile as he approached Gabriel, who was grinning back at him.

"Hey bud," Gabriel said as the two embraced and gently headbutted. "You doin ok?"

"I'm doing great," Jackson lied as he pulled away from his brother. "Thank you for doing this for me, I think it really helped."

"Really? You mean it?"

"Yes, I really do. I'm sorry was such a prick about it, it was the booze and the.... you know. *Him*."

Gabriel hugged his brother again, harder this time, and Jackson swore he heard his voice break. "We will get through this together, I promise. I love you. I have your back forever."

Jackson was disgusted at the false display of affection coming from his brother, but sticking to the plan, he played into it. Hugging his brother back, he whispered softly, "I will make it up to you Gabe, I promise.'

"You don't need to do anything for me, you are all I care about."

"No, no, I insist," said Jackson, grinning. "It will be for your own good."

# SIXTEEN

The National Crime Information Center, or NCIC, is the Federal Bureau of Investigation's primary criminal database. It contains criminal histories, stolen property, missing persons reports and fugitive information. The purpose of the NCIC is to allow Federal, State, and local law enforcement to run someone or something (firearm or vehicle) and to receive instant feedback on its status in the criminal justice system. Whether it be a driver's license status or an active warrant, the NCIC gives police much-needed access to quick information and has become an invaluable tool to all law enforcement.

At the request of Detective Blackthorne, Detective Adrian "Lemon" Meyer had run several names through the National database and was returning the information to his friend and colleague. Glenn sat at his desk checking emails, when Detective Meyer entered his office with a stack of papers and sat them near Glenn's keyboard.

"Ok, I got histories on Kristen Ramierz, Johnathon Temple, Tamara Shard and Isabelle Crix. I don't know why you couldn't do this yourself," Detective Meyer said.

Without hesitation, Glenn responded, "Well, it was about time that you actually did something around here."

Meyer chuckled a deep smokers laugh. "Glenn, you are one big pile of shit. Wait, no, that's degrading to shit. How about a, *"Thank you, Detective Meyer for helping me"* or *"I couldn't do it without you, Adrian,"* you know. Something like that."

Glenn didn't look away from the computer screen. "Thanks Lemon. I appreciate you."

Detective Meyer grumbled at the mention of his nickname and turned about to leave the office when Glenn stopped him.

"Lemon, I need your opinion on this case I'm working." Meyer sat down in an open chair in front of Glenn's desk. "What's up?"

Glenn looked away from the computer monitor and to the pile of papers that Detective Meyer had set in front of him. He picked a few of them up and started thumbing through them.

"I caught a missing person last Friday before my interview. It was actually just before I stepped outside and talked with you. Anyway, the caller was the sister of the missing party, and she gave me her information and blah blah blah, but the weird part is that when I was doing some follow up work with the coworkers, I called one of them and they seemed really distressed over the phone and never called me back. That person is also my main suspect and was really close to the missing party."

"So?" Lemon asked. "This seems pretty straightforward there, Glenn. I mean, first of all, why the hell are you taking a missing person's case? You are homicide and missing persons have nothing to do with you. Second, do you have any proof that this suspect was involved other than being friendly with the missing person?"

"I don't have shit, to be honest with you," said Glenn. "And I took the case because it seemed like a good idea at the time. The woman I called, Tamara Shard, was the person I was told last saw Isabelle, the missing party, before she actually went missing. She won't return my calls and ever since my incident with Scott, I have noticed that I am second guessing myself and I guess I just wanted a second opinion on the matter."

Lemon nodded understandingly. "Glenn, the incident with Scott was a really messy shit show, and I know it's been a tough row to hoe. With that being said, as your friend, you really need to sort this shit out. You are an excellent investigator and have made some outstanding cases, but you are no good to any of us when you second guess yourself."

Glenn knew he was right. He hadn't felt the same confidence in himself after the arson case and knew that he would be a detriment to the team if he couldn't keep his head and his ass wired tight.

"As for the case," Lemon continued, "I looked at the NCIC reports on the people that you had me run. One of the names stood out and it was that Tamara Shard lady you mentioned. It sounds like you are on the right track checking her out, since she does have an active warrant for possession of narcotics. Whether or not she is involved with the missing person, you can at least snatch her up and take her to jail for the warrant. That may be just enough for you to get some confidence back and get back to being the old Glenn. The one that knew how to make the tough calls."

Glenn smiled at his old friend. "I guess you're right. Thank you. And if you tell anyone about this conversation, I will tell everyone about how you wear heels at the truck stop on Friday nights, turning tricks."

Lemon laughed again. "Glenn, my only client is your mother."

The men laughed and shook hands. Glenn's phone began to ring, and Detective Meyer excused himself from the room. Glenn fished his cell out of his pocket and looked at the caller ID.

*MARY BLACKTHORNE*

Glenn had forgotten that Mary had been out of town for the weekend and was excited to talk to her since their fight. Glenn answered the phone.

"Hey, Love. How are you doing?"

"Hi Glenn," Mary said, her voice sounding very concerned. Glenn was now alarmed.

"Everything ok?" He asked.

Mary was quiet for a second. "Ummm… I guess so? I had just returned to the house and as I was walking up to the front door, when…" Mary's voice trailed off. "When what?" Glenn asked.

"Glenn, a little girl just fell out of our trash can."

## SEVENTEEN

"A what?!" Glenn asked incredulously.

"A little girl just fell out of our trash can!" Mary repeated. "I walked up to the house and the trash can tipped over and scared the hell out of me, and a little girl crawled out! She was terrified and was asking me for help and said she knew you?"

Glenn still couldn't comprehend what he was hearing.

"Www…" he started. "Who is she? What does she want? Is she ok?"

Glenn could hear Mary asking the girl questions and heard the muffled responses.

"She says her name is Santina. She said that she is in trouble and needs your help," Mary said. "Glenn, what the hell is going on?"

Bewildered, Glenn tried to answer. "I have no idea. I met her at the playground the other day when I went for a run. She's the girl that's always on the swing, remember? I just told her if she ever needed any help, that I'm a police officer and told her we lived over here. I was just trying to be nice; I didn't know she was actually going to show up."

Glenn could hear the little girl crying on the other end of the line. "She's really upset, Glenn. She says something bad happened and she needs to tell you about it."

Glenn signed and rubbed his temples. "Ok. Take her inside and make her comfortable. I'll be home in a little bit. Do her parents know she is out?"

"She won't stop crying!" Mary exclaimed. "I don't understand what she is trying to tell me."

"Ok, ok," Glenn said. "I'm on my way."

Glenn navigated the rush hour traffic as quickly as he could, but it still took him over half an hour to get home from the office. The sky was getting dark when he finally pulled into his driveway and shut the vehicle off. The entire ride, he tried to imagine what would cause this girl to hide in the trashcan at a stranger's house. He opened the front door and saw Santina sitting on the living room couch with one of Mary's quilt blankets draped over her. She was drinking some hot chocolate and seemed to have calmed down. Thor was sniffing at her inquisitively, and Mary was gently rubbing her back when they all noticed Glenn.

"I finally got her to relax," Mary said. Thor barked excitedly and ran over to Glenn, whimpering and nuzzling his hand for a head rub. He quickly greeted the massive dog before pushing him away. Glenn walked over to Santina, and she looked up at him with puffy eyes and a sore, red nose. Glenn knelt next to her and studied the discoloration on her throat.

"Santina," Glenn said softly. "Are you ok? Tell me what happened."

Santina avoided his gaze and looked down into her lap.

"Santina. Tell me what happened," Glenn asked again.

"Heeee heee huuurrt mmmeeee," Santina stuttered.

"Who hurt you?" Glenn asked.

Santina was quiet again. Her eyes began to fill with tears as she remembered what she saw.

"Santina, you need to tell me who hurt you," Glenn said.

"Jaacckson did," Santina struggled.

"Who's Jackson?"

Santina could no longer control herself and the tears flowed freely.

"I saawww hiiimm in the baaaassseee, the baaaassseeeemeent with a muh muh monsterrr and mmmmommma was thh there and he was tewwing it to… to feet," she blurted.

Glenn could not understand what this child was trying to tell him. Her stutter was exacerbated by her distraught state, and it was very difficult to decipher what she was saying.

"He what?" Glenn said, puzzled by the young girl's response.

"He tooooold it to feeeeet," Santina whimpered.

"I don't understand," said Glenn looking at Mary who was just as confused as he was.

"FEET, FEET, FEET!" The little girl cried.

"Easy, easy!" Glenn cooed. "Who is Jackson? Does he live with you?"

Santina nodded.

"Ok, you said he hurt you? Where did he hurt you? Is it your neck?" Glenn wrapped his hands around his own neck to demonstrate.

Santina nodded again.

"You said Jackson hurt your mom too? Where is she?"

Santina closed her eyes. The disturbing images of what occurred in the cellar played over and over again like a carousel spinning across her mind.

"Ssssshe's dead," Santina whispered.

Glenn was stunned. "How do you know that?"

"Sssshe was wif the monnnster," Santina said.

"Hmm. A monster huh?" Glenn asked. "Santina, tell me where you live."

"1513 Meeeadow luh luh lane."

"So just up the street from here?"

"Yyyes."

Glenn stood and looked at Mary again, who had resumed gently rubbing Santina's back and Thor began licking her tears, he could tell something was wrong. Mary's face was distraught and visibly concerned and Glenn motioned for her to join him in the kitchen. Mary joined Glenn in the kitchen and made sure they were out of earshot of Santina.

"What do you make of all this?" Mary asked.

Glenn shook his head. "I have no goddamn idea what is going on. I don't know if she is telling me the truth or if she is a runaway with a dramatic story or she is off her medication." Glenn peeked around the corner and saw that Santina was still sitting on the couch in her blanket, the giant dog demanding ear scratches. "What I can tell you is, the marks on her neck are recent and are too large for her to have done to herself. I am just going to over to her house and talk to the parents and check the situation out."

"That doesn't sound like a good idea, Glenn! What if she is telling the truth and someone in her house has been killed!" Mary reasoned. "Besides, shouldn't you call someone on patrol instead of going by yourself?"

Glenn frowned. "Mary, the resources on patrol are limited as is and I can't justify if this situation is worth their time, just yet. It's better if I go take a look and if I need them, I'll call." Glenn stepped out of the kitchen and back into the living room. Santina was deep and thought and when he knelt next to her again, she hardly noticed his presence.

"I'm going to go up to your house and check on everything. What's your mom's name?" Glenn asked.

Santina sniffled. "Tuh Taaamaraa Shard buh buh but everyone calls her Tammy."

Glenn felt the wind leave his lungs. This was the daughter of the elusive Tamara Shard who had last seen Isabelle Crix a week ago. Now, her daughter shows up at his home and says strange things are going on. Glenn knew that he needed to pay a visit to the house.

"I'll be back in a little bit. If I don't call or return home in about an hour, then you can call the calvary. Remember, I'll be at 1513 Meadow Lane."

Mary nodded. "I guess we will just sit here and watch a movie or something while we wait!"

"Nnno dooon't go!" Santina screamed, startling the adults. "Jaaaackson will huuurrt yyyou."

Glenn smiled at Santina. "Nobody is going to hurt me; I'm just going over to talk. That's all. See if we can get this mess sorted out."

Santina started to protest but Mary intervened. "Sweetie, are you hungry? Let's go into the kitchen and have some supper."

Santina huffed. *Why don't the adults ever listen to me?* She wondered as she followed Mary into the kitchen, Thor close behind.

Glenn watched as the pair disappeared and when they were gone, he slipped silently out the front door. The sky was near black, and the moon was completely visible when Glenn parked his vehicle outside of 1513 Meadow Lane. Glenn looked out the window at the little house and noticed that it had seen better days. The paint was fading, and the windows were quite dirty. It appeared that the steps of the front porch had also been destroyed at some point. The house didn't have a porch light but there was a glimmer of light coming from the inside. Glenn checked his belt for his badge and pistol before stepping out into the night.

Glenn walked to where the porch steps should have been and navigated the heap in order to knock on the front door. He rasped the old door twice with his knuckles.

No answer.

Glenn struck the door three more times; this time he could hear movement inside.

"Who is it?" A voice barked through the door.

"Tulsa Police. Open up, we need to talk," Glenn ordered.

The door cracked and Glenn could see a mountain of a man covered in tattoos looking at him through the partially opened door.

"Prove it," the man said.

For what felt like the millionth time in his career, Glenn pulled his suit jacket back to reveal his badge and prove that he was a police officer.

"Are you Jackson?" Glenn asked.

*How the fuck does he know my name!* Jackson thought.

*"The girl told him!"* The Third hissed.

Jackson opened the door all the way, his large frame filled the doorway. "What did I do this time?"

"Nothing that I am aware of at this point," said Glenn. "But I did want to ask you and Tamara about Santina. See, she came over to my house earlier and she told me quite the story. I just wanted her parents to know that she is ok, but I wanted to get your side of it too. May I come in?"

*"He knows too much!"* The voice whispered.

Jackson thought about it for a moment. "Sure. Why not. Santina and her mom got into a big fight earlier and Santina ran off. I'm sure glad you were able to find her! Come on in, make yourself comfortable. Sorry bout the porch, damn thing fell apart on me yesterday."

*"He knows! She told him! Get rid of him!"* The Third demanded.

*"Shut up, I have an idea,"* Jackson thought. *"I'm going to figure out how much he really knows."*

Glenn climbed through the front door and into the small living room. It was tidy and clean, and everything sat nicely in its own spot. Jackson pointed to an open chair at the kitchen table for Glenn to sit, while sitting down himself. Glenn sat in the chair across from Jackson.

"I'll be brief," Glenn said to the immense man in front of him. "Santina came to my house earlier and scared the hell out of my wife. When I spoke to her, she said that you had hurt her and that there was a dead body in the house."

Jackson howled with laughter. "That girl! She has quite the imagination! She argued with her momma about some shit, and I spanked her for it! That's all! And as for dead bodies, there are no dead people here! Like I said, she has a wild imagination and I'm sorry you had to deal with it."

"She seemed genuinely upset when I saw her," Glenn said. "And do you have an explanation for the marks on her throat?"

"Marks? What marks?" Jackson asked.

"There are marks on her throat like she had been strangled. She says you were the one who did it."

Jackson tensed. "I don't know nothin about no fuckin marks on that kid's neck! I just spanked her earlier, is all."

"Uh huh," Glenn said. He was watching Jackson's face as they were speaking. The large man had a tendency to look away briefly when answering Glenn's questions, a good indication that he was lying.

"And where was Tamara during all this?"

"She was on the couch," Jackson stated, pointing at the couch. "Are you trying to accuse me of something here?"

"Where is she? I'd like to talk to her," Glenn said.

"She's asleep," Jackson lied, shifting uncomfortably in his chair.

"I thought she worked evenings and nights at the gas station?" Glenn said, trying to catch Jackson in a false statement.

"She does, she just…uh…has the night off." Jackson's eyes were now way too shifty for Glenn's liking.

"I don't believe you," said Glenn. "Another issue I have is that I tried calling Tamara earlier and she sounded like she was being coached over the phone. I'm assuming it was you telling her what to say."

"Fuck you. Get out of my house," Jackson said angrily. He did not like the direction this conversation was going, especially since he had gone to great lengths to keep his activities secret.

Glenn gripped his pistol discreetly. "Listen guy, I just had a young girl hide in a trash can at my home, scare my wife, tell me a wild story and so I decided to come over here and see what happened. While I have been talking to you, you have given me inconsistent answers and your body language indicates that you have lied most of the time."

Glenn leaned across the table. "Tell me what is going on and I will remember your cooperation."

Jackson smirked. "First off, you have no evidence of anything, so eat shit. You also have no probable cause to search my home or arrest me. Second, I don't have to talk to you if I don't want to, so I want a lawyer. You legally cannot ask me anymore questions."

Glenn chuckled. "Actually, that's where you are wrong. I have a young girl terrified of you, saying that you strangled her, and she also claims that there is a dead body in this house. You're absolutely right, I don't have enough probable cause for a search or arrest, however, I DO have enough reasonable articulable suspicion that a crime has been committed and I can detain you while I get a warrant to search this property."

Glenn stood; his hand wrapped tightly around the grip of his sidearm.

"Stand up, turn around, and put your hands behind your back."

Jackson stared at him.

"Stand up, now," Glenn ordered.

Jackson stood and faced away from Glenn, his hands to his sides. Glenn moved swiftly to Jackson's back and pulled his handcuffs from a small holster on his belt. He shoved Jackson to the wall and pulled his enormous arms to the small of his back before applying the handcuffs.

*I should really get someone else over here,* Glenn thought as he removed his cellphone from his pocket and scrolled through his contacts, keeping one hand securely on Jackson's arm.

He was distracted just long enough for Jackson to drive his huge body backwards, catching Glenn off guard. Jackson swung his head as hard as he could and caught Glenn across the jaw; the force of the massive blow knocked Glenn unconscious and he tumbled to the floor. The exertion caused Jackson to fall on top of Glenn's body, but he quickly scrambled to a seated position next to Glenn. Jackson wasted no time, and by scooting backwards on his rear, began to search Glenn's pockets blindly with his restrained hands.

*No key.*

"Fuck," muttered Jackson as he re-positioned himself to his knees. He placed the top of his head in Glenn's ribcage and inched himself to the tips of his toes. Driving with his powerful legs, he flipped Glenn to his back and returned to the search for the keys. The detective was stirring at this point and Jackson knew that he didn't have much time. Sweat forming on his forehead, Jackson finally found the tiny handcuff key in Glenn's front pocket and fumbled it behind his back to unlock himself.

Glenn started to wake up. He groaned as he came back from his concussive state and immediately felt the swelling on the left side of his face. The blow from Jackson's battering ram of a head had loosened a couple of Glenn's molars and he could taste blood in his mouth. He opened his eyes, and everything was blurry and all he could hear was a deafening ringing. He made out the shape of a huge man sitting next to him, struggling with something behind his back, but his vison was still faulty. Glenn saw the figure pull his hands from behind his back and rub his wrists. The figure stood over him like a menacing shadow and the last thing Glenn saw before returning to darkness was a giant boot heel coming down on his face.

Santina was worried. Glenn had not come home yet, and as far as she knew, Mrs. Blackthorne hadn't spoken to him on the phone since he left. The were both on sitting on the couch with bowls of chocolate chip ice cream in their laps, watching tv.

"Mmmmrs. Bwaackforne?" Santina asked.

"Call me Mary, sweetheart." Mary said with a warm smile.

"Mmary? Mm mm miiister guh Glenn doeesn't haaave a key."

"Glenn is a police officer Santina. He knows what to do. I'm sure he will be home in no time at all. So, try not to worry," Mary said, trying to keep her own concerns invisible from Santina.

*It's been nearly an hour, and he hasn't called.*

"But," Santina started "Buut hee cannt get inn wifout a keey. I haaave a keey."

"Don't even think about it," Mary said. "Glenn is a very capable man, and I wouldn't feel comfortable with you leaving the house this late, especially after what you have told me. Please don't worry, everything is ok."

Santina didn't feel like everything was ok. Deep down she felt like something awful had happened and Glenn needed her help. She tried to push the feeling aside, but it continued to crowd her thoughts and she couldn't even enjoy her ice cream.

*He needs a key to get in and get Jackson.*

They sat in silence and watched mindless television and tried not to think about Glenn. After their show was over Mary stood from the couch.

"I have to use the bathroom really quick. Would you like some more ice cream when I get back?"

Santina nodded and Mary smiled. She had always wanted a daughter, and as strange as the circumstances were, she felt happy that Santina was in her home.

Mary shed her blanket onto the couch and walked down the hall to her bathroom. Santina waited until she heard the door close before jumping to her feet and putting her shoes on. She grabbed her backpack and quietly opened the front door. She had to push away the curious Thor who woofed at her as she tried to leave. She allowed the door to close shut and disappeared into the night, moving quickly down the street towards her home.

*Mister Glenn needs me. I have the key.*

# EIGHTEEN

Lieutenant C.J. "Tuck" Tucker took his left hand off his weapon and held up a fist, signaling for the team to stop. The SWAT operators immediately froze in place and kneeled, facing outwards to pull security, eyes and weapons scanning for threats. Tuck took a knee as well and keyed up the microphone to his radio.

"Reaper team, this is Odin, give me a sit-rep," Tuck whispered into the hand mic mounted to his shoulder. The two-man sniper team known by their call sign as "Reaper" was comprised of Collin Bostwick, who manned the midnight black Remington 700 sniper rifle and his spotter, Jed "Mac" McKenzie, the senior member of the reaper team. Both men were dressed in camouflage uniforms and perched atop an out of use city building, facing a neighborhood where a disheveled white house stood, slightly illuminated by the moon in the dark night. The Reapers had been ordered to gain overwatch of the target house when they were first briefed and had moved independently of the rest of the SWAT element when they all arrived on scene.

Jed McKenzie slowly keyed his mic. "Odin, we have visual on the structure, one pickup truck with its headlights on, facing the west side of the house. Windows are boarded and we do not have a clear line of sight inside."

"Any sign of the suspect?" Tuck asked.

"Negative," his radio crackled.

"Copy all."

Tuck looked back at his team and gave the signal that they were moving again. The men were silent as ghosts as they slinked down the alleyway adjacent to a row of houses. Each was an elite member of the Tulsa SWAT, highly trained, and willing to undertake dangerous assignments that no other law enforcement personnel could handle. Utilized in situations of extreme risk of life, the SWAT operators were the tip of the spear when it came to a tactical solution of barricaded subjects, high risk warrants, and active shooters, among many other assignments. They were equipped with top-of-the-line gear and received multitudes of specialized training throughout their careers, creating a lethal pairing of technology, muscle, and skill. A rigorous selection process ensured that the members of the SWAT team were no ordinary cops, but the Tulsa warrior elite who could take on the physical and mental stresses of the job, and, most importantly, win.

Their mission tonight consisted of a violent felon named Emillio Florez, who violated the terms of his parole and snuck out of the state- run halfway house, stole an idling vehicle, and absconded to his sister's home two miles away. When the sister threatened to call the police on him, he stabbed her fatally, which drew the attention of the neighbors, who in turn, called the police. When officers arrived, the subject had barricaded himself inside and said he would start shooting at anyone that approached the house. A negotiation team had successfully failed at coaxing the man from the home, and now Tulsa SWAT was at bat. Highway Patrol and Tulsa Police had blocked the roads to prevent oncoming traffic, and, at the request of the tactical team, power had been cut to the home the suspect was barricaded in.

Tuck and his six-man team continued through the alley, scanning all yards and windows, sweeping their weapons as the passed fences and dumpsters to ensure they were clear, and finally staging near the back fence of the home, staying low and out of sight. The night was incredibly dark and even with the porch lights of neighboring houses, the house was difficult to see, and since the power had been cut off, the inside of the home was devoid of any light; just the way the Tulsa SWAT liked it.

Tuck turned to his team.

"Prepare to breach."

"Moon's out, Goon's out," Mike Davos, the team breacher, said as he lowered his night vision goggles from his helmet to his eyes. The rest of the team followed suit, making sure their infrared lasers attached to their suppressed weapons were on and visible through the night vision. The team prided themselves on being able to "own the night" when the situation called for it, and the affectionate term of "goon" was referring to those in a tactical operator capacity.

"Keep it tight, watch your corners. Dynamic entry, let's go. Bull, cover us as we cross this fence."

"You got it, boss," Dean Graybull said, dutifully covering the team's infiltration with his rifle. The other operators carefully began scaling the four-foot chain link fence in front of them, and with silent precision, entered a single file formation to assault the house. They crept through the yard, and every operator's weapon was trained on a different window as they approached the back door of the two-story home. Even through their night vision, the team could see the paint was peeling off the outer walls and the warped wooden back porch creaked as their heavy gear laden bodies stood on it. They peered through the pitch-black windows and weren't able to see anything, or anyone, inside. The men pressed tight to the wall in a single file line, known as a "stack", and moved to the door, careful not to stand directly in front of it.

A dynamic entry was a typical *shock and awe* breach into a building, usually where the door was kicked or knocked down, and the operators swarmed inside quickly in order to catch their targets by surprise. It was extremely effective when surprise and speed were the best course of action, and the SWAT team were experts at it. Tuck took his hand off his weapon and pumped his fist up and down.

*Breacher up.*

"Big Mike" Davos, so nicknamed for his immense size and strength, left his position in the stack and removed a compact Remington 870 12 Gauge breeching shotgun from his back, and the hulking man quickly scurried across the doorway and onto the other side of the frame so that he was pressed against the wall and looking at the team.

Tuck was the second man in the stack and tapped the shoulder of the man in front of him, a short, wiry man by the name of Shane Gibbons. Gibbons removed a flashbang from his grenade pouch and stood ready for the command. Tuck nodded to Davos and Davos nodded back, before reaching for the door handle with his large hand and seeing if the door was unlocked. It wasn't. One of the procedures Davos had learned at breacher's school, was to ALWAYS check the door handle, because it is much easier to walk in rather than to knock it in. Davos then quickly scanned the door frame with his fingertips, searching for any wires or clues that the door was rigged with explosives. When satisfied, Davos leaned again on his side of the wall and awaited orders.

A silence then fell over the group, as if they were all in a trance, programmed like machines, fearless and willing. It seemed as if time slowed down, and they all forgot how to breathe. It was the calm before the storm. Tuck looked up and gave Davos the signal.

Davos nodded and swung his shotgun to the striker plate of the door and fired a breaching round into the locking mechanism, effectively blowing it apart. "Big Mike" Davos then kicked the door so hard, that the rusty hinges snapped, and the door clanked across the floor and disappeared into the jet-black house. Shane Gibbons pulled the pin on his flashbang grenade and threw it inside.

"Bang away!" Gibbons cried, before stepping away from the doorway, so as not to be affected by the flashbang. The grenade activated with an incredible *bang* and flash of white light. The intended use of the tool was to stun and disorient a room or target in a non-lethal capacity, thus allowing SWAT operators to get the upper hand.

With laser like focus, the team entered the house, sweeping left and right with their weapons. With clock like precision, Tuck and the SWAT team cleared each room in the downstairs of the house, and quickly stacked near the staircase to conduct the second half of their assault. They resumed their usual stack positions, except for one, Jesse Childers, the junior most member of the team, who now was the point man.

The staircase was in two parts and had a landing that attached to a hallway, but the landing was also a vantage point to look down at the operators, and that's exactly what Emillio Florez was doing. In his left hand, he held a Sig Sauer P226 9mm pistol, and was aiming it over the railing at the staircase that the team would be advancing from. He had made it this far and he refused to go back to prison, no matter what the cost.

Tuck tapped Childers' shoulder and said, "Let's go." Tuck signaled to the rest of the team that they were moving and slowly, they began their ascent up the stairs. Childers kept his weapon trained forward instead of up towards the landing, it was an uncommonly foolish mistake that Flores planned on exploiting. As soon as the operators were in view, Florez began firing his pistol blindly and the operators collapsed on the staircase trying to avoid his shots.

"Contact!" Childers yelled as he was hit in the neck and head and collapsed to the floor. Tuck raised his weapon and fired three rounds into Florez's chest; Florez dropped his weapon and fell back onto the ground, out of sight of the team. The team medic, Charlie "Doc" Nelson, drug Childers back down the stairs while Tuck and the operators went upstairs to ensure the threat was neutralized. They reached the top of the staircase and kicked the pistol away from Florez and put him in handcuffs, a procedure to make sure that the suspect could not reach for other weapons, even if they were dead. Tuck and the team cleared the upstairs bedroom, where Florez's sister had called from and saw no sign of her. They swept the remaining rooms and found no other targets and proceeded back to the staircase where Gibbons was pulling security on Florez's body. Tuck reached for the mic on his shoulder.

"Command, this is Odin. House is clear, suspect is down. One operator is down, how copy."

Tuck's radio crackled to life. "Copy all, Odin. End exercise and prepare for debrief."

"10-4," said Tucker into his radio, before addressing the team. "All clear, end of exercise."

Florez stirred on the floor. "Will somebody *please* get me out of these fucking cuffs? You gorilla's tightened the shit out of them." Gibbons removed a handcuff key and unlocked the handcuffs before assisting Florez to his feet. Florez rubbed his wrists and winced in pain.

"Goddamn, guys. Not only does Tuck shoot me three times, then you try to break my wrists with those cuffs!"

Tuck smiled. "You deserved it. It adds character."

Florez scoffed. "Right, like you would know anything about character. Good shootin' though, I thought I had you for sure. Who was that on point? They fucked up big time, he didn't even look at me while I was leaning over the railing." Sergeant Emillio Florez was another member of the Tulsa SWAT team and had been selected to play the opposition for the training mission.

Tuck sighed. "It was Childers. By the time I saw his mistake, it was too late, you had already started firing at us. You killed him, by the way, shot him twice."

"FNG," Florez replied. *Fucking New Guy*.

"He's still learning," Tuck said. "If I remember correctly, when you first joined, you misjudged a flashbang deployment, and it bounced off the door frame and got all of us instead of the bad guy inside."

Florez smirked. "Who, me? Couldn't be."

Gibbons wasn't fazed. "L.T, it doesn't matter if he is learning, that shit, in a real-world scenario, could not only have gotten him killed, but the rest of us too. This unit has too much responsibility to have fuck ups like that."

Tuck turned to Gibbons. "I am well aware of the gravity of the situation, Shane, having been a SWAT member for twelve years. You guys focus on your jobs and let me worry about training the new guys, understood?" Tuck said sternly, making it abundantly clear that *he* was in charge.

"Understood, sir," Gibbons said.

"Good. Now, let's go downstairs and debrief."

Gibbons, Florez, and Tuck proceeded downstairs where the rest of the team had assembled, chatting excitedly about how the operation had gone down. When Tuck approached, the voices quieted down in anticipation of what their leader was going to say. Tuck removed his helmet, revealing his dark brown hair with silver streaks, and used his free hand to wipe the sweat from his forehead. Since it was a training operation, the operators used simulation rounds in their weapons; a paintball like munition that could be fired from their weapons with a different bolt assembly. In order to use them safely, special masks had to be worn to mitigate damage to the face and eyes. Tuck removed the mask from his face and slung it into the pile that the others had started. The fresh air felt good on his hot skin, and he looked at the row of burly hunters in front of him. The Reaper crew had left their overwatch position and were making their way through the doorless doorway. Tuck cleared his throat before he spoke.

"Alright. First off, good work. In all, everything went as smoothly as I could have hoped. Reapers, good work gaining overwatch so quickly, as you know, it is vital that we have eyes on the target before we approach, so, you nailed it."

The Reaper's bumped fists, and the sniper, Collin Bostwick spoke up. "Could have got there sooner, though. We damn near died on that rickety piece of shit fire escape ladder. The damn bolts were starting to come loose."

The group chuckled at the remark and Tuck turned their attention back to the debriefing. "Regardless, good job. Where's Big Mike?" Mike raised his hand, and the group began chuckling again.

"Jesus Mike," Tuck said. "What did that poor door ever do to you?"

"It said something about my momma. It needed to go," Mike Davos said with a toothy grin. The only black man on the SWAT team and at six foot four and three hundred pounds, Mike had played as a defensive lineman for Oklahoma University and was a shoe in as the breacher. He could make anyone, or anything, move out of his way.

"Well, remind me to never say anything about your mother," Tuck said, looking at the splintered door laying on the floor. "Solid breach. I promise, next time we are gonna let you use the detonation cord, and we will have an explosive entry." Big Mike's smile grew even broader.

Tuck looked at Florez. "From the opposition's standpoint, how did it look?"

Florez looked at the group and back at Tuck. "Overall, it was flawless. The power was cut, and it was harder for me to navigate the house, which is good. I didn't even know you guys were stacked up until Mike smashed the door. I hauled ass upstairs and found a firing position at the top of the landing." Florez glanced at Childers. "Once you guys were on the stairs, however, that's when shit got weird."

All eyes turned to young Jesse Childers, who stood stoically against the steel eyed glares that he was receiving from his teammates.

Tuck nodded. "Right. That will be addressed as well. Gentlemen, it is critical that every knows everyone else's job. That way, God forbid, if something happens, someone can jump in and take his place. Next time, if you are unsure about your assignment, trade places with someone who knows it better."

Childers spoke up. "I knew my job, I just got excited. Can't fault me for that right? It's not like you guys don't make mistakes. It happens to everyone."

"If you knew it, then why did you fuck it up?" Dean Graybull snapped.

"Fuck you, kiss my ass," Childers retorted.

"Alright, alright, enough!" Tuck said, silencing the bickering. "Gather your gear and meet outside, Command is going to want to debrief with all of us as well."

The team began shuffling out of the house, when Tuck motioned with his head for Childers to follow him. Childers sighed; he knew what was coming next. Lieutenant Christian James Tucker was a former Army Ranger with eight combat deployments under his belt and another eighteen years with the Tulsa Police Department, twelve on SWAT. He was a highly educated and adept man who took his work as serious as any leader could. As a leader, he found it wise to "praise in public and admonish in private" which was the opposite of what he saw in the Ranger Regiment. Tuck studied leadership teachings from Marcus Aurelius, General George Patton, and Napoleon Bonaparte. He believed that a leader needed to inspire his men rather than belittle them and break them down. However, as with all things, there were exceptions.

Tuck and Childers stepped into the bedroom that was closest to the back door, and Tuck waited for the rest of the men to clear out of the building. Restless, Childers made the mistake of speaking first.

"Lieutenant, about what I said, I…"

"Shut up," Tuck said cutting him off. "You listen and you listen good. You are the newest member of this team, and I gave you a chance, even though you didn't score as high as others. I saw that you had fire in you, a drive that makes a SWAT member special. Next time I try to teach you how to do better, you shut your fucking mouth. I don't care what you think or feel, you fucked up. In a real-world application, you would be dead, and you could have gotten me killed, or worse, one of the other guys."

Childers shifted uncomfortably. Although Tuck was his peer, he had an aura of "father figure" surrounding him and he felt like he was getting his ass chewed from his own dad.

"Sir, I apologize for speaking out of line, but-"

Tuck cut him off again. "Remember that part where I said to shut your mouth? How bout you start practicing now. I have no room on this team for someone who can't follow instructions. So, as penance for your indiscretions, you are in charge of cleaning all the gear tonight."

Tuck's cellphone vibrated quietly in his pocket, and he removed it and saw the caller ID. He quickly accepted the call and put the phone to his ear.

"Detective Meyer! How are you doing my friend?" Tuck said warmly, keeping his eyes fixed on Childers.

"Hey C.J., how's it goin? Whattia up to?"

"Nothing much, just finished up a training exercise, working on the debrief now. You remember how that goes, right? You miss SWAT yet?"

"Yes and no, my body hurts more and more, but I still miss knocking down doors. Listen, I have a favor to ask of ya."

Tuck turned away from Childers. The concern in his friend's voice had piqued his interest. "Sure thing. Whattia need?"

"My colleague's wife just called me and said her husband was investigating a possible child abuse and a possible murder. She said that he hasn't called or returned home when he was supposed to. Do you know Detective Glenn Blackthorne?"

"Only by reputation," Tuck said. Like all cops, he had heard the story and rumors surrounding Glenn and Scott Shoemaker. "Wait, he went in alone? He didn't have anyone go with him?"

"Unfortunately, no. Glenn has had a history of being a bit of a loose cannon at times, so he went solo. I was hoping that if shit went sideways, you guys could go check it out, it would save time from a beat cop showing up and then eventually calling you."

Tuck couldn't believe it. *A cop going to a potentially dangerous scene alone? What a fucking moron.*

"Alright," Tuck said. "Where are we going?"

# NINETEEN

Glenn awoke to see Jackson's face in front of him. Jackson slapped him and Glenn tried to defend himself, but his arms wouldn't work. When Jackson slapped him again, he tried to stand, but he was unable to move. He looked down and saw that he was in a metal chair; his arms and legs were bound with thick, sturdy ropes. Jackson smirked as he fidgeted with Glenn's pistol, he had no doubt relieved Glenn of when he was unconscious. Wherever they were, it was dimly lit from a small candle on a table behind him and there was an incredibly awful smell that saturated the air. The candle's flickering glow cast shadows in front of him and the only parts of the room that he could see were those that were in the orb of light that the candle created.

Jackson stood tall and walked behind Glenn to the table where the candle was sitting. Glenn could hear the rustle of a toolbox opening and closing and Jackson reappeared in front of him, brandishing a pair of needle nose pliers.

"Now, Mr. policeman, it's my turn to ask some questions," Jackson cackled as he put the pliers in one of the nostrils of Glenn's nose. Glenn jerked his head away from the instrument, but Jackson forcefully held him still and reinserted the pliers.

"You're a real piece of shit," Glenn yelled, struggling against Jackson's grip. "A real fuckin scumbag. I'll kill you as soon as I'm free, I swear to God."

Jackson smiled. "There's no God down here."

Jackson took the slack out of the jaws of the pliers to where they were snug against Glenn's tender nostril. "Who else knows about Santina?" He asked.

"Fuck you," Glenn said defiantly. Jackson squeezed the pliers tight, and Glenn cried out in agony. Jackson twisted the pliers to cause more pain and held on to Glenn's thrashing head.

"You're going to tell me what I want to know!" Jackson screamed in Glenn's face.

The sound of rustling chains stopped Jackson and he removed the pliers from Glenn's nose and looked behind him. The chains dragged softly across the floor and a strange squishing noise emanated from the darkness. Glenn strained his eyes but could not see. After being knocked out twice and have having his nostril nearly torn off, his cognitive ability was less than optimal, but the eerie sound of chains was enough to get his attention.

*Something else is down here.*


Santina had successfully made it back to her neighborhood without being followed by Mary. She used the shadows of the night to creep up close to her house. She didn't hear anything the closer she approached, and the front door was closed. The lights were off inside, and all appeared to be normal, but Santina knew nothing was normal about this wicked house.

She slowly moved to the back of the house, hoping to see Glenn on the other side, but he wasn't there.

*Jackson got him!*

Santina was terrified. Never in all her life did she ever think that she would be involved in something so depraved and awful. She was just a shy little girl who liked to swing, why did this have to happen to her? She stood at the front door trying to calm her nerves. *I don't know what to expect in there, but I can't let Mr. Glenn die.* Mustering her courage, Santina opened the door to the one place she never wanted to return, and bravely went inside.

Jackson turned back to Glenn, an unsettling fire in his eyes. "Ohhh now you've done it. You've woke him up."

Glenn was confused by what his captor meant. *Was it a dog or something?*

The candle wasn't powerful enough to light the part of the room that the chains were moving in. The chains were stirring with more vigor now, and the squishing noise got louder. Laughing sinisterly, Jackson returned to the table behind Glenn and picked up the candle and began walking slowly to the source of the noise. The glow of the candle left Glenn, and orbited Jackson as he walked further into the darkness. Glenn could see the beginnings of a large chain on the floor and as Jackson walked further, the horrifying truth revealed itself to him.

In front of Jackson, was a monster. The creature could have once resembled a man, but its pale skin and bony body were grotesque in the candlelight. It had a bushy beard and sunken eyes, and the hair on its head was patchy and gnarled. Its skin was covered in lesions and sores that oozed and smeared across its gangly body. The creature was rolling like an animal in the bloated, rotting human corpse it slept on, creating the stomach-churning squishing that Glenn was hearing. The feral man sat up and growled at Glenn, its thin lips flashing hideous black teeth.

Glenn had never been so petrified in his entire life. The gruesome scene before him caused his heart rate to skyrocket, his breathing became shallow, he could not take his eyes off the creature in front of him, no matter how desperately he wanted to. The beast crawled out of its human bed, and started slowly walking on all fours towards him, like a wolf stalking its prey.

Jackson grinned as he watched his creation move towards its next victim.

"Detective, I like to introduce you to my brother, Gabriel."

Santina could hear sounds coming from the cellar. Just a few seconds ago, she thought she heard the cry of a man in immense pain. Her fear that Glenn was in trouble outweighed her own, and she ventured forward into the dark house. She looked through the door down into the cellar and could hear Jackson talking to someone. The basement was poorly lit, and she could not make out any details. She crept slowly past the door and entered her mother's bedroom, looking for anything that she could use against Jackson and the creature that he kept down there. She quietly fumbled in the dark until she wrapped her hand around a long hard object behind the door. Santina slowly pulled the object towards her and recognized it as Jacksons baseball bat. She had seen this bat before when he had hit that one visitor, they had but hadn't seen it since. She grasped the bat in both hands and carefully walked back to the cellar entrance. She took a deep breath and gently began walking down the murky staircase.

"See, Santina wasn't lying to you when she said there was a monster in this house," Jackson said as he walked back to Glenn. The creature now stood on two legs and walked with a nightmare inducing hunch, arms draped in front of it, following its master. Jackson returned the candle to the table and stood next to Glenn who was fixated on the foul sight that was ambling towards him. The chain went taught and the beast shrieked when it could get no closer. It clawed at its collar with long fingers and jagged untrimmed nails, resembling those of a bird of prey. Even from three feet away where its advance had been stopped, Glenn could smell the odor of the beast and the remnants of the black and green corpse that it mired in. Its soulless eyes pierced Glenn and he could no longer hold back his disgust and vomited on the floor next to him. Jackson was pleased to see that his brother had the desired effect on the Detective. Glenn spat and inhaled deeply before looking back at Jackson.

"What kind of sick fuck are you!? To keep this thing down here? And you said it was your brother?!"

Jackson's smile had vanished, and he spoke flat and harshly. "What are you expecting me to say? To regale you with my life story? I'm sorry to tell you, that it is too long of a story for someone who won't be around to remember it."

Glenn played for time; he wanted his captor to be distracted while he figured out a way to escape. "Hey, man," Glenn said. "You've got me tied up in your basement, the least you could do is answer my question."

Jackson laughed. "You know what, ill indulge. This is my greatest secret. For years, a little demon inside my head has told me to...*do things*...to people. My brother was no exception. He claimed that he had a little demon too, but neither me nor The Third-that's what we called it- believed him." Jackson looked at the ghoul that was now snarling angrily at Glenn. "When we were just kids, we killed a drifter that our mother had brought home. After he was dead, my brother tried to convince me that he still had the darkness in him, and he began cutting the man's fingers off and we ate them together. Gabriel enjoyed that part more than I did, but I can still feel the power that was awoken inside me, and I have been chasing that high ever since."

"But...why would you keep this...*thing* down here!" Glenn asked as he watched the creature foam and drool on its filthy facial hair.

"Gabriel was false. He was jealous of my strength, and he needed to be controlled before he tried to pull one over on me. I found out later that The Third had played us against each other to see who was the strongest. Over the course of our teenage years, he and I were in and out of jails and mental hospitals. When I was in one of the hospitals, The Third and I came up with a plan to keep Gabriel quiet, without me having to kill him. So, I decided that he could become my pet; A vicious deformed version of himself, bound to me forever, and never out of my control. For six years now, he has been my companion in this state. Oh, it took some adjusting at first, he tried to kill me after I first chained him to the wall of our first house, but keeping him deprived of sun and human contact, other than my own, has made him become very…shall we say…loyal? He respects and fears me now. I am his master, and The Third is mine."

"You are insane!" Glenn hollered, his voice hoarse. "That doesn't make any sense at all! You can justify it all you want but you are nothing but pure evil!"

Jackson's smile returned. "Maybe, maybe not. What is evil about what I do? I have no other reason to kill people and to chain my brother like a wild animal, other than that The Third wills me to do it. I have learned not to question my orders, just like a soldier is conditioned not to question theirs." Jackson paused and scratched his bald head. "I've enjoyed our chat, truly, but unfortunately for you, your little friend Santina interrupted his feeding time earlier."

Glenn's stomach leaped into his throat. He now knew what Santina had been trying to tell him before. She wasn't saying feet. She was saying *FEED*.

Glenn strained desperately at the ropes on the chair but couldn't move at all. Jackson looked at his feeble attempt to escape and scoffed. "There's no use in trying to escape, Detective. Once you are down in the cellar…you're gone." Glenn felt all hope abandon him as Jackson moved toward Gabriel's collar and started to unfasten it. All at once, a sickening crack sounded in the basement and Jackson pummeled to the ground. Behind him, little Santina

Shard was breathing hard and shaking while her small hands gripped a large wooden baseball bat.

The monster screamed and began tearing again at its collar, distraught at what happened to its master. It viciously snarled and reached for Santina, who had to jump back to avoid being grabbed by the foul creature in front of her.

"Santina!" Glenn called, "Santina, find something sharp to cut these ropes! Do it NOW!"

Gabriel shrieked and growled as Santina ran to the table behind Glenn and frantically searched for a cutting tool. The tabletop was sparse, so she opened the toolbox and dumped it, the tools scattered noisily across the table and floor. One of the tools, an orange box cutter, skidded past Glenn's feet and stopped inches away from Gabriel's reach.

"Santina, hurry!" Glenn cried as he struggled against the ropes. Gabriel was thrashing violently against his chains and contorting his body in sickening ways to try and escape. Santina continued to look at the pile of tools in front of her.

*Nothing sharp!*

She looked back at Glenn and saw Gabriel's gnashing teeth biting at them. Santina also saw the box cutter lying just inches away and decided to go for it.

"Don't go near that thing, find something else!" Glenn pleaded but Santina was focused on the box cutter and carefully crept to try and reach it. She knelt and extended her arm as far as she could reach but she was not close enough. She crawled closer, cautiously keeping out of reach of Gabriel's outstretched arms. With fingertips, Santina was able to inch the box cutter closer to herself until she could grasp it in her hand.

"I got it!" she cried. Santina tried to stand but, in her haste, she lost her balance and fell forward slightly, now within reach of the wretched feral beast. Gabriel flailed wildly and gripped tightly around Santina's forearm and dragged her closer. Santina screamed as the creature muscled her towards it.

"Let her go!" Glenn screamed as he violently shook in his chair, the bonds still not loosening.

Santina tried to crawl, but the creature was too strong and as she tried to pull her arm away, the grotesque Gabriel sunk his jagged, rotting teeth into her arm. Santina screeched as Gabriel continued to bite and tear at her arm which now was red with her blood that streamed onto the floor. Not knowing what else to do, Santina raised her free arm, and with a mighty cry for courage, jammed her thumb into the monster's black, lifeless eye.

Gabriel shrieked and fell backwards, letting go of Santina's bleeding arm. Acting quickly, Santina scrambled to her feet and grabbed the box cutter that she had dropped. She ran to the back of Glenn's chair and cut hurriedly at the ropes that bound him.

"Good work!" Glenn said once he was free and shedding the ropes onto the floor. Glenn stood and quickly looked at Jackson who was now stirring and holding the back of his head. Glenn could see that his service pistol had fallen out of Jackson's pocket, and he dove for it sliding on his stomach to reach it. Gabriel had recovered, and his new wound filled him with enough rage that he clawed at his collar again, this time breaking his fingernails as he tore it from his neck. Gabriel charged Glenn; his primal roaring filled the basement until it was stopped with three explosive concussions from the barrel of Glenn's pistol. The creature screeched an ear-splitting cry and fell to its knees, bleeding profusely. Glenn transitioned from prone to a kneeling position like he trained a hundred times as a soldier and re-acquired the demon in front of him.

*POP POP POP!*

Glenn accurately delivered three more shots to Gabriel's sternum and the creature released a raspy wheeze as the air exited his lungs before falling onto its face, lifeless, a pool of dark blood oozing from beneath him.

"NO!" Jackson screamed jumping onto Glenn's back, knocking him forward and forcing him to drop his gun. Glenn rolled quickly so he could face his attacker, but he was met with a heavy fist crashing on the bridge of his nose and Jackson pinning him to the ground. Glenn instinctively reached and grabbed Jackson's wrist as he was trying to strike him again.

"You killed my creation!" Jackson cried as he began hitting Glenn with his free hand.

The blows were powerful enough to bounce Glenn's head off the concrete floor, dizzying him and affecting his motor skills. Glenn knew that his attacker was too strong for him to out-muscle but maybe he could out leverage him. Utilizing a Brazilian Jiu Jitsu technique called "the closed guard", Glenn secured his attackers wrists and wrapped his legs around the trunk of Jackson's body, locking his ankles in the back. Glenn now controlled Jackson's hips and therefore controlled his movement. Jackson viciously swung his arms, trying to free himself from Glenn's grip. Glenn pulled Jackson's torso on top of his and while simultaneously gripping Jackson's left wrist with his right hand, Glenn released his attacker's right arm and reached over top of his shoulder and under Jackson's enormous arm, grasping his own wrist, locking it in tight. Even though Jackson struggled, Glenn was able to then force Jackson's hand to the small of his back, and by dragging his opponent's wrist up his back towards his head, created an extremely painful joint lock on Jackson's shoulder. The *kimura*, a Jiu Jitsu shoulder submission, allowed the defender to apply immense pressure to their attacker's weak shoulder joint, ultimately snapping it with little effort. Glenn positioned himself to further execute the technique, when Jackson did something unexpected.

Jackson roared at the excruciating pain in his shoulder and slowly reached with his free hand down to his boot and removed a thin, black handled boot knife. Jackson whipped the knife back up and stabbed Glenn in his exposed underarm. Feeling the blade enter his arm, Glenn yelped and let go of his submission. Capitalizing on Glenn's mistake, Jackson shot up right and stabbed downwards, plunging his knife deep into the detective's leg. He rapidly removed the blade and brought it down a for a second assault, this time when he pulled it out, a bright red spray of blood followed along with it. Glenn cried out and released his hold around Jackson's body.

Jackson raised his knife again and sliced Glenn across the face, blood spurted freely from the open wound on his cheek.

Glenn's face was cut, he had a femoral arterial bleed in his left leg, and Jackson had stabbed him earlier in his tricep. Glenn felt the world going black as the hemorrhaging artery in his leg continued to drain his life force. Glenn was helpless when he saw Jackson raise the knife again, gripped tightly in both hands, the fire from the candle gleaming in his eyes.

"You killed my brother! Now I will kill you!"

Jackson leaned back to strike the final blow but ceased when he saw Santina standing six feet in front of him and extended in her tiny hands, was Glenn's pistol, pointed right at his head.

Jackson was bewildered to see her; he had forgotten that she was in the cellar with them until now. Jackson slowly reached his hand towards her.

"Give me the gun," Jackson ordered. Santina shook her head. Glenn groaned on the ground; he was succumbing to his wounds now. Jackson carefully stood to his feet, not taking his eyes off the little girl that was now threatening him.

"Give me the gun, girl," Jackson growled.

Santina looked down at Glenn, he wasn't moving anymore. Santina was trembling and the pistol bounced up and down in her hands. The fight between Jackson and Glenn scared her so badly that she had wet herself in the affray.

Jackson stepped toward her. "Put the gun down, Tina."

Santina stopped trembling. Her face contorted into a scowl of anger. Her fear had evolved into a great hatred for the monster that stood in front of her. Santina felt her courage rise up again from the depths of her soul.

"Only my momma called me Tina," she said stoically, as she focused her aim. "And you *killed* her."

Jackson snarled and lunged for the gun. Santina squeezed the trigger twice, just as Jackson leapt towards her, the bullets struck the center of his chest and throat. Jackson stumbled backwards and tripped over Glenn, clutching the spurting hole in his neck. He thrashed on the ground, gurgling on his last breaths.

*How…* He thought, *How could this…little…girl …*

Jacksons movements slowed until he laid silently on the floor, dead.

Santina dropped the gun and ran over to Glenn who was still on the floor. 'Glenn! Glenn! Wake up!" She cried as she shook his body. Glenn grunted and opened his eyes slightly to look at the little girl who was shaking him.

"Kneel," He whispered as he lifted his head off the floor. "Kneel on my leg."

Santina quickly scaled across Glenn's bleeding leg and put all other weight on the wound. The outside pressure caused the blood to stop spilling out.

Glenn nodded in approval. "Take my belt off…" his voice trailed, "take my belt and wrap it high on my leg…. make it tight, tight as you can." Santina unfastened Glenn's belt and began pulling it through the loops until it got stuck on his pistol holster.

*I have to hurry!* She thought as she tried to free the holster from the belt. Finally, the holster slipped free, and Santina was able to wrap the belt high and tight on Glenn's injured leg. She sat there panting, continuing to put pressure on his leg.

*What do we do now?* She wondered.

"Thank you," Glenn said. "Thank you for helping me."

Glenn's eyes were heavy, and he laid his aching head back down onto the floor. His strength was gone, and he slipped into darkness on the cold basement concrete. The last thing Glenn's blurred vision saw was four magnificent white balls of light, bouncing down the stairs towards him.

"Angels. The angels are here." he said, smiling, as he faded away into nothing.

# TWENTY

Glenn opened his eyes. He was blinded by white walls and a fully drawn curtain in a small room. He was lying in an uncomfortable bed and looked around and saw an I.V. bag dangling over top of him and the tube protruding from his right arm. His mouth was dry and swollen, and it hurt to move any part of his body. He was wearing a strange one-piece gown and there were fresh bandages on his leg and arm. Glenn sat up slowly in his bed.

*I'm in a hospital.*

Glenn rubbed his temple and winced when he felt the stiches on his left cheek. "Jesus Christ," he mumbled as he remembered the events with Jackson and Santina. As he recalled his harrowing ordeal, Detective Adrien Meyer stepped into the small hospital room, holding a cup of coffee and some vending machine donuts. He smiled broadly at Glenn when saw that he was awake.

"You know, I'll be damned if those stiches didn't actually improve your face," Meyer said as he sat in a chair next to the bed.

Glenn managed a weak laugh. "I guess I won't be winning the *Miss Oklahoma Pageant* this year, huh." Meyer took a sip of his coffee and opened the bag of donuts. "No. But people could use you during Halloween to decorate their yard."

Glenn laid back down in his bed. He hurt too much to sit upright and hoped that a drip of morphine would be coming soon. He turned his head and looked at his friend who was dunking a donut into his coffee.

"How did I get here, Lemon?" he asked.

Meyer took a bite of the soggy donut and chewed. "Mary called me. She said that something had happened to you, and that you went to this little girl's house and then the little girl went missing, and that you didn't call or come home." He dunked his pastry back into the steaming black liquid. "Fortunately for you, I got a friend who's a lieutenant on the SWAT team and they were doing some night operation training nearby. I gave em a call and they hit the house; just in time too, they said when they got downstairs you were nearly dead." Meyer pulled a second donut and began dunking it. Glenn tried to remember the details of the incident.

"I thought I saw angels coming for me in that basement. White lights coming to take me away."

Meyer coughed on his donut. "Yeah," he said, recovering from his misjudged swallow. "If the angels you are referring to have SureFire Tac lights mounted to suppressed MP5's." Glenn knew now that he was saved by the Tulsa SWAT team and not by ethereal beings.

"Where is Santina? The little girl?" He asked.

Meyer continued chewing on donuts and sipping coffee intermittently. "She's fine. Mary asked if Santina could stay with her until everything got sorted out and I said that was fine, especially since that girl aint got any family anymore. She got a nasty bite mark on her arm, but the hospital was able to take care of it. You, however, flatlined twice on the table when the ambulance was bringing you here. You lost a lot of blood, and no one thought you were gonna make it." Meyer paused. "And, like usual, you disappoint me and refuse to die."

Glenn couldn't help but laugh heartily. Despite the pain, he was relieved to know that he has a friend who had his back and that he could call on, anytime, no questions asked.

*The Thin Blue Line remains strong.*

"And in case you were thinking you were gonna get all the glory, you are sadly mistaken." Meyer said, catching Glenn off guard.

"What do you mean?" Glenn asked, his curiosity taking over.

"I solved your missing person case for you. See, after SWAT and the paramedics got you out of there, I went over and worked the scene, and lemme tell you, that was a goddamn mess my friend. I don't know what the fuck you all were doing down there, but it was a forensic shitstorm. We were able to identify three of the four bodies that were there, one of them being Isabelle Crix. She was the one that was bloated and deteriorating. The sister had a hard time dealing with the news. Tamara Shard was still going through the process of rigor mortis when we found her in a different part of the basement, and the third was that Jackson guy. His alias was Jackson Elliott, but when we fingerprinted him, it came back as Jackson Trunt, and buddy, that guy had a fuckin messed up history, I tell you what."

Glenn rolled his eyes.

"Yeah, I figured that one out on my own when he tied me to a chair and tried to feed me to his feral brother that he chained up in the cellar." Glenn said.

"So that's who that was? We couldn't get an ID on that…thing. Its teeth were so jacked up and after years of being chained up like that, it destroyed its own fingerprints," Meyer said, happy that he was able to reach a conclusion of the mystery body.

"Lemon, this all would have taken weeks to get done, how long have I been here?" Glenn asked, his brain couldn't fathom the length of time that had passed since the incident.

"Dude, you've been in here for six days," Meyer said as he finished the last of his coffee. "Like I said, you were almost a corpse when they got to you. That little girl had applied just enough pressure to your artery to make sure you didn't die. The surgeon had a hell of a time fixing you up. I don't envy you when you get *that* hospital bill."

Glenn didn't care about the bill. He was just thankful that he was alive. Detective Meyer stood and stretched his back. He then grabbed his trash and dumped it into the trash can on the other side of the room.

"All jokes aside Glenn, I'm glad you are still with us. You narrowly escaped death and you helped a little girl and stopped an evil piece of garbage. You don't need to prove anything to yourself anymore. You're a good man. Now if you'll excuse me, I don't think I can look at your face any longer without vomiting my snack," Meyer said with a wink. "You need anything you let me know, ok?"

Glenn reached out his hand and Meyer took it with a firm grip. They shook hands in silence. No words needed to be said because they both knew. Meyer turned to leave, and Glenn spoke up. "Actually Lemon, there is something you can do for me." Meyer stopped and turned back to his friend. "As if I haven't done enough for you?" He said jokingly. "What do you need?"

"I need you to call Kimmy Lee for me and have her meet me here. I'm ready to talk about Scott again. I'm not afraid of it anymore." Meyer nodded his head. "I can do that." He flashed a coy smile to Glenn.

"Wouldn't want anyone to think I don't do anything around here."

Over the next two days, Doctors monitored Glenns recovery in the hospital and Santina and Mary visited him whenever they were allowed. The surgery on his leg was healing well and his other knife wounds had not caused any significant damage. He was concerned however, about how people, namely his wife, would react to the large scar that snaked from his lower lip to his earlobe. The stiches were itching him like crazy and he was ready to be done with them. He was able to ambulate but needed a cane to help him do so while he recovered, a new development that he didn't much care for, since it made him feel like an old man.

The day before he was to be released from patient care, he was eating lunch in his room, when Kimmy Lee knocked on his doorframe. As gorgeous as ever, she sauntered into his room and grinned a sexy, pearl white smile.

"Well, hi there, Glenn," she said as she sat in a chair and crossed her legs.

Glenn wiped his mouth and swallowed before greeting her. "Hope you don't mind if I finished my lunch while we talk." He used his fingers as quotes when he said "lunch".

Kimmy giggled sweetly. "Of course not, you should have told me, I could have brought you something more palatable."

Glenn grimaced at his tray. "I'd kill for a cheeseburger right now. Much more of this crap and I will regret they brought me back to life."

"Don't say that!" Kimmy said, putting her hand on his. "We are so glad that you are still around. The news team and I were thrilled to hear that you made it out alive. We did our report on it, and it was a big hit. Lots of interested people. Some publishers have even reached out to us to help try and get ahold of you."

"Publishers as in…for writing a book?" Glenn asked. The idea never would have crossed his mind.

"Of course! Who wouldn't want to hear the story of the hero cop saving a little girl and killing the bad guys!" Kimmy said excitedly. "I know it could be a bestseller."

Glenn considered it for a moment. "You think it could sell?"

"Absolutely!" Kimmy said.

Glenn picked at his boiled carrots and thought. "It's an interesting idea. I'll look into it when I'm out of here."

"You should," Kimmy said as she reached into her purse and removed the small recording device that she kept with her. "Detective Meyer told me that you were ready to finish out interview about the arson, is that right?"

Glenn nodded. "You bet. Besides, I have new nightmares to dream about now. Scott is an old memory at this point." Kimmy placed the recording device next to Glenn and pressed the red button.

'Detective Blackthorne interview, part two," she said aloud to the little black box. Kimmy looked at Glenn who put his tray to the side of his bed. "Are you ready?" Glenn nodded and Kimmy sat upright.

"Detective, the last time we spoke, we were interrupted before we could conclude the interview. We left off where you were telling me about your former colleague, Scott Shoemaker. If I remember correctly, you had just told me that after the pathologist's report, Scott called you and asked you to meet him at the scene of the fire, is that correct?"

"Yes," answered Glenn.

"Tell me more about that." Kimmy said with anticipation.

Glenn thought back to the phone call four weeks ago.

"Glenn, I need you to meet me at the Wabash trailer right now," Scott urged. Glenn rubbed the sleep from his eyes and checked the time. "Scotty, its ten o'clock, what's going on?" Glenn asked, concerned by how frantic his friend's voice was.

"Just do it. I… I have to tell you something," Scott said as he hung up the phone. Glenn turned on the lamp on the nightstand next to his bed and Mary whimpered at the introduction of the light.

"What's going on?" She asked in a sleepy voice.

"I don't know," Glenn said as he climbed out of bed. "But it doesn't sound good."

"After the call, I met Scott at the Wabash trailer park. He was standing in the rubble of the burnt trailer, and he had a bottle of whiskey in his hand. He was disheveled and his collared shirt was untucked. He looked like hell," Glenn said to Kimmy.

"Thanks for coming," Scott said as he took a belt off the bottle of bourbon. He wiped his mouth with the back of his hand and offered the bottle to Glenn.

"No thanks," Glenn said, closely watching his friend. "What is going on Scott? Why are we here?"

Scott stared at the pile of rubble where the two girls were found. "What are your nightmares fueled by, Glenn?" Scott asked. He swayed back and forth, apparently drunker than Glenn thought. "Mine are caused by this fire."

"Why?" asked Glenn.

"Because. I didn't know they were there." Scott took another drink.

"Scott, its time you tell me the truth. You have been acting so weird after this fire and now we are here in the middle of the night, and you are drunk, talking very cryptic. So, pretty please, tell me what the hell is going on."

"Scott told me the truth about the fire," stated Glenn. Kimmy leaned forward, waiting for the big reveal. "He was having an affair with the woman that lived there, Kelly Snow."

"Oh my God!" Kimmy exclaimed.

"Yeah, wait till I get to the rest of it," said Glenn.

"Wait, you've been cheating on your wife with this woman? How long?" Glenn asked bewildered.

"About a year," Scott said. "My marriage was on the rocks, and I met Kelly at a coffee shop where she worked. We started talking and we got along so well that it just…evolved. It soon got physical, and I knew that she was starting to get feelings for me."

Scott finished the bottle of whiskey and threw it in the rubble in front of him, the glass shattered everywhere.

"She wanted me to leave my wife for her. She threatened to tell everyone what we were doing if I didn't leave Carrisa. If Carrisa left, she would have taken my whole retirement, and I would have been fucked. I had to do something."

"Scott told me that he was in a difficult place between his mistress and his wife. Instead of working it out like a functioning adult…he lit her trailer on fire," Glenn said. Kimmy was wide eyed in disbelief.

"You're kidding!" she said.

Glenn shook his head. "I wish I was. The worst part about it though, was that those little girls were Kelly's daughters. Scott didn't know they were in the house when he burned it."

"Now you know why I had to do it, Glenn! She was gonna ruin everything that I worked so hard for. I made sure to clear myself of any of the evidence, but when the pathologist said there were semen traces, I panicked and called you. You gotta help me out of this."

"What?!" Glenn exclaimed. "How the fuck do you expect me to help you, Scott? You murdered three people, two of them were little girls! You can't expect me to help you after something like that."

"We have been friends a long time, Glenn. This is what cops do, they get each other's back right? The thin blue line! I made a mistake and you're my brother in arms, my partner, my FRIEND! We can get through this together, we just gotta get our story straight and make sure no one goes looking in places they shouldn't."

Glenn was furious. "How dare you try to use our friendship to try and use me to cover for you! What you did was wrong, Scott, wrong! Those people didn't deserve to die just to save your fucking retirement. The Thin Blue Line is reserved for those of us that have honor and integrity, not to cover for their mistakes or crimes."

Kimmy was silent. Her eyes willed Glenn to continue the story.

"When I refused to help Scott, he got very quiet. The gravity of his deeds was starting to weigh upon him, and he knew he had no way out. I was fully intent on arresting him until…"

"Go on," Kimmy urged. "Until what?"

"Scott knew that I had no choice but to arrest him, I mean, he just admitted to killing three people in an arson, for crying out loud! When he saw that I wasn't going to help him, he pulled his gun on me." Glenn's eyes went misty. "I told him to drop it, but he didn't listen, so I had to shoot him. I shot him twice and he died instantly." Glenn wiped his eyes with his bed sheet. Kimmy was empathetic and dabbed at her eyes with a Kleenex, trying not to smear her makeup.

"Scott was my best friend," Glenn continued. "We worked out together, trained together, and arrested bad guys together. He taught me how to be a cop. He was always there when I needed him, but I couldn't return the favor on this one. He had gone too far, and I wasn't going to allow that. A lot of outsiders had something to say about how it all went down, like I was a traitor to the cause or something, because I didn't back a fellow officer. There will always be evil in the world Kimmy, and there will always be a need for cops, but what we don't need is officers that are morally corrupt and won't stand for the right cause. There is so much scrutiny on law enforcement nowadays and it is getting harder and harder to get support from the populace we defend. Every time you turn on the news, there is another cop getting in trouble for something and a department that swore they had no idea of it happening. I'm not sure who actually said it, due to it being disputed, but one of my favorite quotes is, *"The only thing necessary for evil to triumph, is for good men to do nothing."* I am not a hero for stopping Scott. I just didn't want to be the one who did nothing."

Kimmy and Glenn were silent as the words sunk in. Finally, Kimmy broke the silence in the room.

"Well. I certainly got a lot more than I expected, Mr. Blackthorne. Thank you for sharing it with me." She reached out to the bed and turned her recorder off and returned it to her purse. She wiped the final tear from her eyes and gave an exasperated smile. She stood and took Glenn's hand.

"For what it's worth, especially in light of recent events, I believe that you are indeed a hero. You have been selfless and courageous, not only with Scott, but with the Trunt case as well. To me, you are one of the good ones in a world that desperately needs trustworthy police. She leaned over and kissed him on the cheek.

"Thank you for keeping us safe."

Glenn blushed, he wasn't expecting a kiss from Kimmy Lee, but didn't mind it either.

"You take care of yourself, Detective," she said as she shouldered her purse. "I'll reach out to you when the interview airs."

Glenn thanked her and she left his room. He was alone now with his thoughts. He was happy that he was able to finally tell the full story of Scott Shoemaker to someone. He thought of Mary and sweet little Santina and what a good life they could have together. He leaned back in his bed and for the first time in a long time, Glenn Blackthorne felt the weight of the world be lifted from his shoulders. He fell asleep and was free of ugly dreams. He was finally at peace.

# EPILOGUE

Glenn was eventually released from the hospital, but it was still too soon for him to return to duty. After he was cleared from the shooting that occurred in the basement, the Tulsa Police Department awarded Glenn the highest honor they could bestow, The Medal of Valor. Glenn graciously accepted the award and the following day, put in his resignation. He had seen too much evil in the world and wanted to focus on his family.

The Tulsa SWAT team had a private award ceremony for the rescue of Detective Blackthorne and little Santina Shard. The ceremony was unexpectedly interrupted when they got called out to assist with a high-risk search warrant. The work of an operator never ends.

The day of Glenn's retirement, he and Mary had surprised Santina with adoption papers, and Santina was so excited and grateful, she cried for three days afterwards. Santina, after standing up to her bullies, had lost her stutter. The courage she displayed in saving a Tulsa Police Detective gained national media attention and she was asked to speak at multiple televised talk shows alongside Glenn. The City of Tulsa even awarded her a ten-thousand-dollar check to be used towards her tuition at any college she wanted. Santina was utterly star struck and was amazed by how much her life improved. Her life had completely changed, and she was revered at her school but students and faculty alike. Sally Mosenteen had finally left her alone at school and since her stutter had disappeared, she had an easier time making friends and communicating with people.

Mary was pleased with how things in her life were going as well. She gave Glenn admonished Glenn harshly about him putting himself in danger, but it wasn't long until she was wrapping him up and squeezing him tightly. She said that if he ever did something like that again, she would kill him herself. Santina was new to her life and Mary felt the fulfillment of being a mother and the supreme joy that it can bring. The two came together so easily, there was hardly an adjustment period and they rarely ever disagreed.

Glenn wrote his book chronicling the events of Jackson and Santina, and it became a New York Times Bestseller in under a month. His publishers demanded another book almost immediately, and he decided to write about Scott and the arson case, changing a few details here and there. The writing was surprisingly natural to him, and he wished that he had started a project sooner. He had a lot of creative ideas that he always wished he could put down on paper, but never got to it.

On a warm Saturday evening, Santina walked into Glenn's study and threw her arms around his neck as he sat at the computer, furiously typing away.

"Daddy, can I go play on the swing set?" she asked sweetly.

"I don't have an issue with it," Glenn said, looking away from the screen and back at her. "Just be home before its dark."

"Ok!" she said excitedly and donned her Zebra coat, the one she always wore, exited the room, and opened the front door of the house.

"Where are you going in such a hurry?" Mary asked, looking up from the novel she was reading.

"Daddy said that I could go play on the swing set!" Santina said.

Mary was filled with joy to have someone in their house refer to Glenn as "Dad."

"Ok. Just be home before dark," she said.

"Yes ma'am!" Santina exclaimed and shot out the door.

Santina walked to the playground full of excitement. This was the first time she had gone on a weekend in a long time, and she was looking forward to solitude. The events with Jackson were always on her mind but she was in theraputic counseling for it now, and it was helping.

As she approached the school, she saw a group of boys hanging out near the fence by the swing sets, and as she got closer, Santina saw that it was Connor Simmons and his buddies. The boys stopped what they were doing and watched as Santina strutted up the sidewalk towards them and through the opening in the fence next to the swings. Connor and his friends giggled as they approached Santina, who watched them carefully as they advanced.

"Hey retard!" Conner said, causing the group to howl with laughter. Santina sat on her swing and stared at the group.

"I betcha that all that stuff we heard about you was made up!" Conner sneered as he got in Santina's face. Santina didn't even flinch when he got nose to nose with her.

"There is *no* way that Santina Shard the Retard, ever helped the cops out or went on tv. It's all a bunch of crap to try and make yourself look good. But I know that you are just the same old stupid…" Santina exploded out of her swing seat and snatched Connor by the collar of his shirt and threw him down hard on the ground. The group of friends were so taken aback, they didn't know how to respond. Connor was crying on the ground when Santina stood over him.

"I'm not scared of bullies anymore, *Connor*. And everything you heard about me is true, so shut your mouth." Santina looked up from Connor and into the group of his wide-eyed friends.

"And it's not Santina Shard anymore, it's Santina Blackthorne!"

Connor Simmons scrambled to his feet crying and ran off, his gang following closely behind him. Santina watched the scared group run out of sight before she sat back down on the swing. She was not at all aggressive, but she did promise herself that she wouldn't be treated poorly by anyone ever again, a promise that she intended to keep.

She pumped her legs, and the swing began to move. She continued gaining momentum until she was satisfied with the height and speed that she was going. While she swung, something unexpected happened; she began to cry. She cried for her momma, Tammy, and for all the other people Jackson had hurt. She cried for the years of torment from bullies and mean kids. Most of all though, she cried for Glenn. If it had not been for him, her life would be over, and she would not be able to enjoy the swing she was currently sitting on or go home to a loving family that cared for her more than anyone else ever had.

Santina Blackthorne suddenly stopped crying and it was replaced with laughter. She wiped her tears and laughed as she began counting the fence posts. She was finally free and now was finally loved. She counted the fence posts and laughed and swung into the evening.

And the swing sang beautifully.

Printed in Great Britain
by Amazon